Trial by Rebellion

Francis Ken Josiah

Llumina Press

© 2007 Francis Ken Josiah

All rights reserved. No part of this publication may be reproduced or transmitted in any form or by any means electronic or mechanical, including photocopy, recording, or any information storage and retrieval system, without permission in writing from both the copyright owner and the publisher.

Requests for permission to make copies of any part of this work should be mailed to Permissions Department, Llumina Press, PO Box 772246, Coral Springs, FL 33077-2246

ISBN: 978-1-59526-696-5

Printed in the United States of America by Llumina Press

Library of Congress Control Number: 2007900762

Trial by Rebellion

"It is not the critic who counts, not the man who points out how the strong man stumbled, or where the doer of deeds could have done better. The credit belongs to the man who is actually in the arena; whose face is marred by the dust and sweat and blood; who strives valiantly; who errs and comes short again and again; who at the best, knows in the end the triumph of high achievement, and who, at worst, if he fails, at least fails while daring greatly; so that his place shall never be with those cold and timid souls who know neither victory or defeat."

Theodore Roosevelt
(Paris Sorbonne, 1910)

Acknowledgment

I invested a lot of time in conversation with many friends and colleagues about this project. The principal motivation to take on this daunting challenge was to unveil the plight of government troops misled by military leaders. While l do not subscribe to violence as a means to a political end, I stoutly denounce civil war as a solution to a man made political problem.

This project came to fruition partly through the efforts and inspiration of Retired Lt. Col. Reginald Glover, Lt. Col. J E Milton, Lt. Col. D B Sowa, Lt. Col Gbondo, Major Momodu Keita, Major Peter K. Lavahun, Airborne Cadets 'Class of '91', of the Sierra Leone Army, Brigadier Zibiri and Captain Ali of the Nigerian Training Group to Sierra Leone, (NATAG).

A very special thanks to US Army Sergeant First Class Kevin O'Grady, WO1 Glen Wharton, Psyops training officer Captain Carlyle, Bete Franken at John F. Kennedy Special Warfare Center and School at Fort Bragg, North Carolina, Professor Ron Fionte at Emmanuel College, Dr. June Speakman and Steve Esons at Roger Williams University, Constitutional Law Professor and Attorney at Law, Mathew Planter III, Esq., Ginnette Brazille, Captain Judith Blackwood of the Jamaican Defense Force, (JDF), Suzanne Hopkins, Abdulai and Jamal Manasaray, the Khaddar family, Catherine Burns, Sam Goba, Aiah Kaigbanja, Haja

Fanta Janneh, Abdulai Rahim, Ali Sheriff, and Mrs. Sousa in East Providence, Rhode Island. And finally, to God be the glory.

Introduction

The object of writing about this piece of history is to revive the memory of all the fallen soldiers, policemen, civil defense vigilantes, and innocent men, women, and children caught in the line of fire during the rebellious civil uprisings in Sierra Leone and Liberia. This book is also an apology to all those who were hurt by combatants.

Sierra Leoneans still bear the scars of the Revolutionary United Front's (RUF) political campaign grounded in brutal violence. The explosion of the civil war partly stemmed from the government's underestimation of the warnings, ill preparedness to deal with the insurgency, and the tactical blunders of the nation's military leaders.

Remotely, the civil war in Sierra Leone was among other things an unconventional political adjudication of the ruling All Peoples Congress (APC) government, by disgruntled dissidents whose patience with the state of economic failure had grown unbearably thin. The preconceived verdict was the eviction of the government from power and the restoration of freedom from the shackles of a twenty-four-year reigning one-party government.

The civil rebellion crippled an already plundered economy, shed innocent blood and tears and facilitated the loss of lives and property worth millions. Expenses incurred for procurement of wartime logistics also milked millions of dollars from the government treasury, with an inestimable percentage of those funds from loans.

Though largely unpopular, the civil uprising, sponsored by Charles Taylor from neighboring Liberia, served as the catalyst that would unveil the long hidden political disaffection that the majority of Sierra Leoneans held against the reigning one-party government. The civil war exposed the chronic defects of the nation's dysfunctional army, and crystallized the collective fortitude and resilience of Sierra Leoneans, who refused to cave in to thuggery, bigotry and warlordism.

The repressed seeds of political consciousness and inquest into years of economic stagnation, were forced to regenerate out of the systemic violence. In his inaugural speech on March 29, 1996, President Tejan Kabbah noted, "during the last civilian administration [referencing the Momoh government], the gates of indifference, insensitivity, inefficiency, and callousness were opened and those traits resulted in the untold tragedies of a senseless war"

In the 1990s, graves opened their jaws en masse along the West African sub-region from Liberia to Sierra Leone, swallowing up soldiers and innocent civilians without discrimination. The RUF abducted and conscripted innocent children, coercing them to take up arms, to fight a political cause whose origin and effect they could not possibly understand.

The civil conflict turned out to be a calculated sales opportunity exploited by weapon manufacturers, in exchange for unpolished diamonds as a form of payment. It seems apparently easier to publicize, condemn and enforce the regulation of conflict diamonds, yet little has been done to apply the same strict regulatory standards to weapons manufacturers, dealers and buyers.

The continued failure of the United Nations to criminalize the indiscriminate sale of weapons to non governmental groups and coercion of children into combat, is a new challenge worth ethical, if not political consideration. This book is dedicated to all those who lost their lives, especially child soldiers all around the world, to the merchandise of unregulated arms dealers. The loss of innocent lives from unregulated sale of arms for profits and selfish political causes creates little or no value for the betterment of humanity.

The conscription, psychological enslavement, physical molestation and subjugation of children to the dictates of socio-political upheavals, are heinous acts begging to question of the depth of concern for children. The case for the countless Sierra Leonean and Liberian children is presented here, leaving parents with nothing to show for the loss of their precious kids, except for these lines, the memories of their immediate families, and the earth that eventually swallowed up their silent remains. If a cause was lost or won, theirs was neither victory nor defeat.

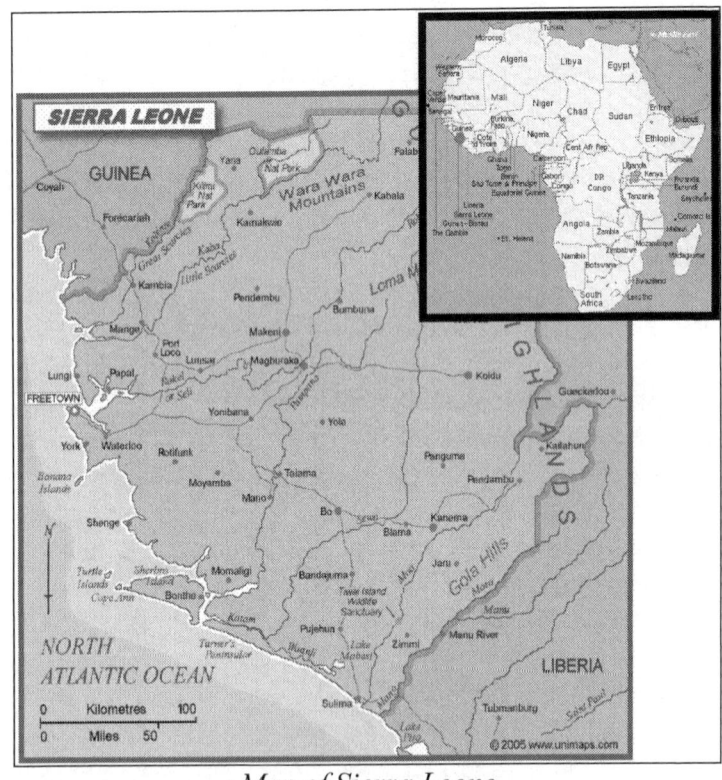

Map of Sierra Leone

Chapter 1

In 1991, the civil war in Liberia had reached a chaotic peak. A quintessential model of third-world anarchy, Liberia was split into fractional portions, with half its territory around the capital Monrovia under the control of the reigning government of Samuel Doe. The other half had been overrun and controlled by Charles Taylor's National Patriotic Front of Liberia. (NPFL).

The Taylor-led NPFL was composed of disgruntled Liberians opposed to Doe's government. Its principal aim was nothing short of overthrowing the government of Samuel Doe.

A Krahn by tribe, Doe was the first indigenous Liberian to hold the office of the presidency, an office he assumed in April 1980 by an effortless coup. Doe occupied a deserted power vacuum following the assassination of President William Tolbert. A descendant of the influential, wealthy Americo-Liberians referred to as *Kongors*, Tolbert had succeeded the late William Tubman, one of a long line of the Kongor minority to rule since independence in 1847.

On the occasion of Tolbert's assassination, Master Sergeant Samuel K. Doe was the senior non-commissioned officer (NCO) on duty at the Executive Mansion, Liberia's official residence of the president.

Master Sergeant Doe occupied a power vacuum vacated by senior Liberian army officers, after scheming President Tolbert's assassination. With the support of his fellow NCOs, Doe translated his bravery into self-appointed leadership of Liberia. He became the first NCO to rule a nation by a coup d'etat and led Liberia's first ever coup as well.

He faced stiff opposition to his rule during his early years in office. Most senior Liberian army officers and Liberia's educated elites, were united in their opposition to Doe's leadership. He survived several attempted coups plotted by senior Liberian army officers who underestimated the support for his leadership.

Charles Taylor entered Liberia's political theater on his return from studies in the United States of America, taking a job in the late President Tolbert's administration. Following Tolbert's assassination in 1980, Taylor was appointed Director of the General Services Agency in Doe's government. Three years later, Taylor was charged with massive embezzlement of government funds. He fled Liberia to the United States of America.

Doe's strong diplomatic ties with the Reagan administration secured him the extradition of Taylor to stand trial in Liberia. In 1985, Taylor mysteriously escaped from the Plymouth County correctional facility in Massachusetts. According to the *Washington Post*, the *Boston Globe*, The Forum for International Policy and the Scowcroft group, Charles Taylor, Prince Johnson, Foday Sankoh and many radicals from Liberia, Guinea, and Sierra Leone surfaced in Libya's guerrilla training camp in Benghazi, to prepare for a major sub-regional political revolution in West Africa.

Charles Taylor's principal aim was twofold; first, to make Liberia the base of support for subsequent sub-regional rebellion and second, to overthrow the government of Samuel Doe through armed civil rebellion as an exemplary model for regional radicals. His tool of choice was guerrilla warfare. The reason: it was a perfect mode of warfare whose complexity defied conventional warfare tactics, regardless of the strength of a conventional army. The tenacity, loyalty and sophisticated weaponry of Doe's army offered little deterrence to the notoriety of guerrilla warfare.

Taylor needed unfettered access to Sierra Leonean, Guinean and Ivorian territories, as supply routes and staging areas for a multi-pronged attack on Doe's army. He solicited help from leaders of Liberia's immediate neighbors, but was turned down by the Guinean and Sierra Leonean governments. Taylor resorted to exploiting the poor relations between the Ivorian President Houphet Biogny and Doe. President Boigny embraced Taylor's cause to undo Doe's government as payback for a domestic feud.

Taylor led his National Patriotic Front of Liberia (NPFL) guerrillas into Liberia through the Ivory Coast border. Liberia's political landscape was divisive and ripe for an uprising. Doe had stepped on a lot of political opponents. It was therefore easy for Taylor to unite the opposition to support him. Taylor's rebellion was remotely an internal power struggle between the Kongors and Gios, versus the Khrans and Madingo tribes. Gio's support for Doe was borne out of the violent execution of General Qwionpka, a renown Gio army officer who had led a force to overthrow Doe. Knowing Doe's ability to subdue dissidents, Taylor was hailed for bravely standing up to the tall autocratic order of Doe's regime.

Taylor ran his NPFL organization from Gbanga in the north of Liberia, staffed by hardline anti-Doe elements. He rewarded supporters with political appointments to fill vacated local government posts and executed opponents with impunity. Taylor governed through a self-appointed civic administration, ran a local radio station and raised supplemental revenue through taxation, diamond mining and looting.

What was perceived by many within Liberia and the sub-region as another of many attempts to overthrow President Doe, initially attracted little attention. Doe's loyal armed forces had built a reputation for containing anti-government uprisings, but Taylor's brand of guerrilla rebellion evolved into a tough challenge to the sophisticated armory of the Liberian army.

Decorated in Rambo-style ammunition belt links, head ties and painted faces, while armed to the teeth with AK-47 Kalashnikov rifles, general purpose machine guns (GPMGs), M16s, British G3s, and nerves of steel, brainwashed and drugged teenagers of the NPFL indiscriminately destabilized towns and villages, executed, raped, conscripted and maimed innocent displaced civilians throughout the Liberian countryside.

Trial by Rebellion

While serving the immediate and long-term political agenda of Taylor's NPFL, the youths of Liberia joined the uprising for its economic rather than its political appeal. The chaos was exploited as a means to an economic end. Looting was the key incentive attracting impoverished, politically disenfranchised youths.

Taylor challenged the authority and legitimacy of Doe's government by attacking Doe's forces, political supporters and government institutions. With Doe's popularity hanging on a thin thread, Taylor's movement won an unofficial referendum as the voice of the people.

Taylor's guerrilla organization and message of political change earned him the leading voice over other anti-Doe forces. Taylor also adeptly utilized the British Broadcasting Company's (BBC) Africa services, as a vehicle of mass communication. Relying on its dedicated African audience and distant outreach, he effectively shaped airtime to garner support and legitimize his call for Doe to relinquish the presidency. Taylor used the BBC as a medium to warn the Liberian people of his intent to remove Doe from the Executive Mansion by force.

With unlimited access to the Ivory Coast and its power base, control of the vast expanse of Liberia's kimberlite diamond fields along the Mano river and the Yekepa mines in Nimba, including the massive Firestone rubber plantations, Taylor held Liberia's economic hot spots hostage.

The direct and swift intervention of the United States in the affairs of its former colony was crucial to the peace and stability of the sub-region. It never materialized. George H. W. Bush's administration refrained from upholding the official support and recognition the Reagan administration offered President Doe.

Liberia's civil war coincided with the Iraqi invasion of Kuwait in 1990-1991. Liberia's crisis like the rest of Africa's was not a priority on Bush's political menu. The liberation of Kuwait from Iraqi occupation took greater precedence and media coverage.

The United Nation's lethargic bureaucracy and snail-paced response to African issues further isolated Doe and the Liberian people, giving Taylor lead time to consolidate his territorial hold on major parts of Liberia. The Liberian crisis evolved into an intricate sub-regional political debacle, provoking and exposing the depth of diplomatic inefficiency and disunity among West African leaders. It resulted in the bloodiest crisis to have collectively impacted the stability of the West African sub-region since independence.

Chapter 2

After five years as military head of state, Doe held multi-party elections in October 1985. Doe shed his military uniform to celebrate his electoral victory under the flag of the National Democratic Party of Liberia (NDPL). He was inaugurated a civilian president on January 6, 1986, amidst opposition from politicians who claimed the results of the elections were fraudulent.

Doe spent his first few years recalibrating Liberia's economic decline. Some argue he made it worse. He inherited a poorly managed economy. In 1979, inflation spiked to a new high and the cost of food increased, sparking a major riot in Monrovia. Demand for Liberian export commodities, especially iron ore, fell significantly draining national revenue.

One of the few African military leaders to officially tread the forecourt of the White House lawn in Washington DC, Doe used the opportunity to propel Liberia from its dismal post-Tolbert economy, to new heights of growth and development. At the height of the cold war, Doe's endorsement of President Ronald Reagan's anti-communist foreign policy, combined with the elections held in 1985, earned him an economic aid package to jump start Liberia's economy.

Liberia's economic boom from sustained trade relations with the United States helped revamp Liberia's ailing economy, transforming Monrovia into a sub-American icon in West Africa. Liberia's flourishing economy attracted migrants from neighboring Sierra Leone, Nigeria, Guinea, Mali and the Ivory Coast. Liberia's maritime infrastructure made her a booming sub-regional market for coveted American-made goods.

At the inception of the Taylor-led war, NPFL rebels were motivated by the need to lay hands on tons of goods docked in Liberia's Freeport. The loot found a marketplace in neighboring Sierra Leone and Guinean border towns. Sierra Leone and Guinean security officers deployed along the border colluded in the illicit trade of looted goods from Liberia.

The long stretch of Gola forest along the Liberian and Sierra Leonean border spanning Koindu, east of Sierra Leone, down the tip of Sulima in the South, remained largely exposed to NPFL rebel trading activities. NPFL guerrillas exploited the bustling commerce along Sierra Leone's border, primarily for its gains and a decoy for pre-war reconnaissance in Sierra Leone.

Taylor's long-term strategic interest in a destabilized Sierra Leone was well known. He wanted to hurt President Momoh for denying him support and access to Sierra Leone's border. He also wanted to secure a share of the diamond proceeds mined from Sierra Leone by installing a puppet rebellion. He recognized that control of the lucrative mineral resources in both countries

Trial by Rebellion

would attract diamond traders to finance his war and fill his own pockets with wealth.

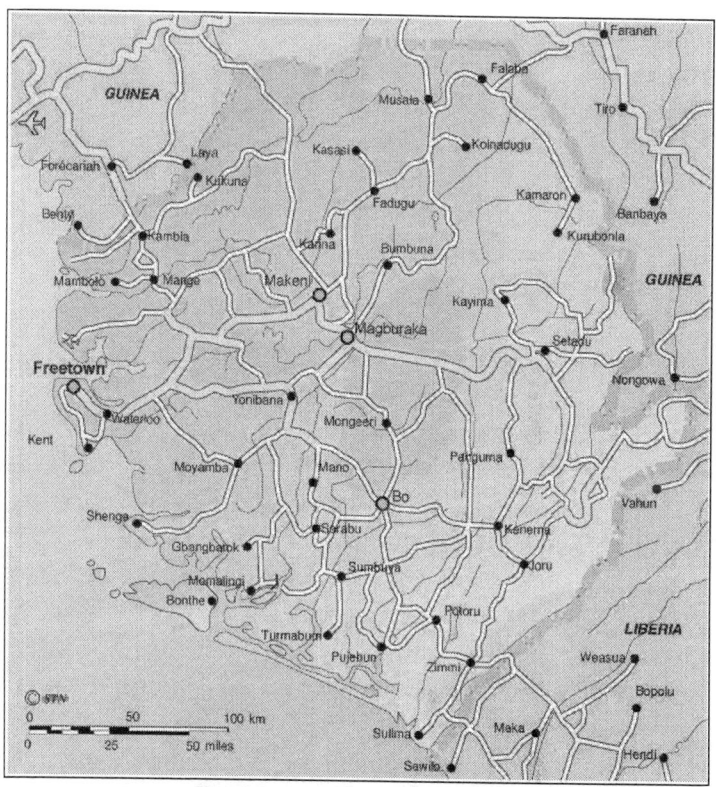

*Tri-Nation Road Network.
Sierra Leone - Liberia – Guinea*

The icy diplomatic relations between Momoh and Doe served Taylor's invasion scheme well. Stronger relations between the two neighboring leaders could have crippled Taylor's uprising at its very infancy. Taylor spent time in Freetown before heading to Ivory Coast to initiate his guerrilla movement. In the course of his brief detention in Freetown, he could have been easily handed over to the Doe government on the strength of an extradition treaty with Liberia. In the absence of such treaty he was released.

Taylor repeatedly advertised his intent to give Sierra Leoneans a taste of civil war. His threats were the earliest indication of his designs to disrupt Sierra Leone's porous security. Sierra Leone's national security apparatus remained unscathed by Taylor's widely publicized remarks.

In the course of the chaos in Liberia, countless intelligence reports of a pending dissident invasion filtered to leaders in Freetown. Sierra Leone's poorly trained and under-funded military intelligence unit relayed the sketchy information to political and military authorities. The intelligence reports were stacked on the shelves and neglected in the rubble of complacency and ignorance.

The army leadership reneged its national duty to proactively investigate the validity of reports of an insurgency. The failure of the political and military authorities to address the manifest threats to the nation's security, reveals the extent of institutional malfeasance and negation of the safety of Sierra Leoneans.

Over the years, the army had been reduced to a political security unit, servicing the ceremonial needs of political pageantry. Sierra Leone had two infantry battalions, the first in Freetown and the second in the northern town of Makeni. She also had a garrison in Lungi close to the International airport, another in

Trial by Rebellion

Daru, in the east, close to the Liberian border. Sub military branches included a logistics depot, army engineers, medical, intelligence, education, communications (Signal Squadron), and mechanical services unit. In addition to these units was a military training center outside Freetown.

Then army Chief of Staff Brigadier J. S. Momoh and his immediate successor milked government funds in the name of maintaining the army. Calculated against the exchange rates in the late 1980s, the average monthly wage of a non- commissioned soldier was equivalent to $2.46 per month. Commissioned officer received any where from $3.36 to $22.03 depending on the rank. When an average senior government official makes no more than $23.03 a month but drives a car or owns a house costing well over $200.000, misappropriation of government fund happens to be the only logical source of extra income. In 1988, defense expenditures minus wages, capped at $6 million, less than one percent of the gross domestic product. The top army brass like its public sector counterparts had perfected their skills at diverting public funds.

Appropriated defense funds were exclusively personalized, circulating around the accounts of the higher military echelon. The nation's defense infrastructure was starved of its immediate and long-term logistical needs, forcing the middle and junior ranking personnel into desperation and poverty.

Troops carried empty, defective, antiquated rifles and occupied dilapidated, overpopulated, unsanitary barracks. Many soldiers resided outside the barracks, commuting to their stations of duty at their own expense. Lack of prospects for professional growth, narrow promotional opportunities and frustrating wages drove many fine junior officers into early resignation. The subsequent depreciation of talent in the army left the institution in the hands of an inefficient leadership, rendering the nation vulnerable to Taylor's invasion.

Chapter 3

By mid-1990, the level of atrocities committed by NPFL rebels in Liberia attracted the attention of the international community, including the regional Economic Community of West African States (ECOWAS). Principally an economic body with the sole purpose of advancing trade and economic interests among its sixteen member nations, ECOWAS leaders shared security concerns over the worsening crisis in neighboring Liberia.

According to the Human Rights Watch, Liberia's refugee population in 1991 was 750,000, a third of its pre-war population spread throughout West African nations. The U.S. State Department's Refugee Bureau reported that in July 1991, there were an estimated 227,500 Liberians in the Ivory Coast, 342,000 in Guinea, 6,000 in Ghana, and 125,000 in Sierra Leone, with smaller numbers in Nigeria, Gambia, and Mali. The rate of fatal casualties from crossfire, disease and malnutrition were inestimable. ECOWAS leaders resolved to take actionable steps.

The United Nations in concert with some western nations, including the United States, gave ECOWAS its blessings to facilitate a possible ceasefire. The intent of ECOWAS was clear, but the mechanics of implementing the ceasefire was not public record.

On August 7, 1990, the desperation of the situation forced a conference of the ECOWAS Standing Mediation Committee in Banjul, Gambia, to decide an immediate course of action. The committee agreed to form a military observer group, the Economic Community of West African States Monitoring Group (ECOMOG), comprising infantry, air, and naval forces, contributed by some member nations.

ECOWAS shared a common interest to resolving the humanitarian crisis, but sharply differed on methodology capable of containing the bloodshed. Member nations were either neutral or took sides along political lines, depending on pre-war relations with Doe. The former French colonies, including the Ivory Coast, Guinea, Guinea Bissau, Senegal, Mali, Benin, Togo, Burkina Faso and Mauritania, held different views than the Anglophone countries. Francophone countries frowned at military intervention, offering to support a dialogue. Former British colonies, including Nigeria, Ghana, Gambia and Sierra Leone, opted for a boot on the ground style intervention.

The multi-regional intervention force under the command of Ghana's General Arnold Quinoo was issued a vague mandate; to restore order in Liberia, create an environment that would allow humanitarian operations, and foster a cease-fire.

Bent on denying ECOMOG peacekeepers a safe entry, NPFL rebels mounted an assault on ECOMOG troops. Overhead air strikes from Nigerian jet fighters could not soften the resilience of NPFL fighters. By its initial reaction to the NPFL's onslaught with equal aggression, the coalition compromised its mission and credibility as a peace broker from the outset.

ECOMOG managed to secure a landing on August 24, 1990, with the tactical co-operation of Taylor's former field commander Prince Johnson, who had defected, forming the Independent National Patriotic Front of Liberia (INPFL). ECOMOG's forced landing into a chaotic, hostile, rebel-infested Monrovia begs to question whether the peace approach was besieged by strategic flaws from the onset. ECOMOG was also eventually compelled by aggressive attacks and growing ECOMOG casualties to transform its mission from peacekeeping to peace enforcement.

Peaceful dialogue was not fully explored as a preamble to military intervention, because sub-regional leaders did not take Taylor seriously, nor did they recognize the enormity of his uprising. Militant intervention alone was not the best organic response to a regional problem with the potential to balloon into immeasurable catastrophe.

A West African peacekeeping force was a novel idea. It was the first of sorts, deployed into a chaotic political and militant landscape, besieged by many unknowns and limited logistical support from almost all its enthusiasts. The formation of the peacekeeping force symbolized a major sub-regional political development, but the scope of its agenda was shaken by alliances that were in conflict with its ultimate objectives.

Sierra Leone offered its airport as a base for servicing ECOMOG jet fighters and reservist forces. Sierra Leone contributed a total of 377 men, comprising three infantry companies and a logistics support unit, to join the bulk of troops, with the greater portion of arms and leadership provided by the Ghanaian and Nigerian contingents.

ECOMOG also encountered logistical insufficiency to support the complexity of peacekeeping. Nations in the sub-region had several domestic economic problems they could not solve much less offer a feasible solution to the Liberian problem. The intervention was hastily planned. Its conceived mission was poorly executed and misguided by inexperienced peace brokers. And, it was mounted against unexpected internal opposition. An inhospitable environment bloated by operational complexity and conflicting political solutions among its political players, ECOMOG was a recipe for failure.

Chapter 4

Peacekeeping military commanders in Liberia were strapped by constraints invented by the political leaders, whose interest they served in Liberia. ECOMOG's effort was smoldered by the sensitive nature of its political objective, the inhospitality of the chaotic combat zone and the warring factions.

Managing Liberia's crisis was the core challenge of sub-regional leaders. Sub-regional ECOMOG leaders were in disagreement over the best solution to Liberia's escalating civil crisis. Dissent revolved around the interest of stakeholders in relations to the interventionist options available to restoring peace in Liberia. Military-style peacekeeping presence was the dominant concept, but the idea had its critics. In truth, the safety and security of the Liberian people caught in the war were accorded little or no comparable consideration to the wishes of the sub-regional political players.

Options available to the resolution of the Liberian crisis ranged from a cautious facilitation of a temporary ceasefire, promoting a forum for intra-factional dialogue and reconciliation, subsequent power sharing through an interim administration, enticing and rewarding restraint, starving the flow of ammunition into Liberia through the Ivory Coast and peace enforcement as a last resort.

Peace enforcement was an oddball that meant full-scale combat with the well organized but recalcitrant NPFL. The best among these options would have been a hybrid canonized by craft and flexibility.

Ivory Coast president, Houphet Boigny was supportive of the removal of Doe and opposed to ECOMOG's militant intervention. Nigeria's leader, General Ibrahim Babaginda and Ghana's Flight Lieutenant Jerry Rawlings were inclined to uphold Liberia's political status quo, meaning preserving Doe's government. Sierra Leone's president Brigadier Joseph S. Momoh had an insignificant voice among his sub-regional peers. He simply played along with the Anglophone military alliance.

In support of the militarist alliance, Sierra Leone offered her territory to the Anglo-military dominated coalition. The Ivory Coast offered hers to the NPFL. Francophone troop contribution paled in comparison to Anglophone troops.

Political pressure from Dakar not to get militarily involved forced Senegalese troops out of the conflict, leaving Guinea as the only major Francophone contributor to the coalition. Guinea was also the only Francophone country governed by a military leader. Captain Blaise Campoare of Burkina Faso did not contribute troops and was supportive of Taylor.

Owing to its dominant military contribution to the coalition, the Anglophone military alliance prevailed in pursuit of an aggressive interventionist campaign. ECOWAS's disagreement over a single feasible solution deterred a unified politico-military strategy on the part of ECOMOG's mission in Liberia.

ECOMOG mismanaged and misdirected its role at the infancy of its operation in Liberia. It failed to quickly contain the crisis from further escalation. Its efforts were rendered further useless following a poorly managed meeting with President Doe. The meeting was cut short by an INPFL siege and abrupt abduction of President Doe under the eyes of ECOMOG commanders. Johnson's rebels brutally decapitated President Doe and dismembered him body part by body part, searing his wounds with salt water from the Atlantic Ocean.

Though unintentional, ECOMOG was wholly responsible for the capture and brutal slaying of Doe. The capture and torture of the Liberian leader, attests to ECOMOG's bogus security arrangement and peacekeeping inexperience. By his death, Doe's elimination from Liberia's power equation dismantled the Armed Forces of Liberia, (AFL), leading to wider political fragmentation. New factions and intra-factional fighting emerged, extending ECOMOG's responsibilities, further complicating an already delicate and unmanageable crisis.

The AFL regrouped as an anti-Taylor faction, forming the Liberians United for Reconciliation and Democracy (LURD). LURD disintegrated into the United Liberation Movement for Democracy in Liberia (ULIMO), one faction led by former Doe government official Alhaji Kroma, the other led by Roosevelt Johnson. George Boley's Liberian People's Council (LPC), also emerged in the factional upsurge.

Adding to the existing chaos, ECOMOG's new challenge was managing its relations with the splinter forces. ECOMOG maintained biased relations with rebel factions, compromising the neutrality of the Nigerian-dominated peace brokerage organ. The West African peacekeeping force resorted to forging odd alliances to suit its tactical convenience. ECOMOG's prejudice towards the NPFL spurred a bitter rivalry. Under the circumstances, peace in Liberia was a long shot.

ECOMOG evolved into another faction, its sole mission -denying Taylor passage to the Executive Mansion in Monrovia. ECOMOG commander General Quinoo ran ECOMOG operations at the dictates of Presidents Rawlings, Babaginda and Nigerian generals deputizing him in the Liberian front.

The coexistence of different armies, each with distinct organizational cultures, language barriers, command and dogmatic views, clashed with the overall objectives of the operation. Nigeria's dominant role in the operations created an unequal balance in the overall decision-making process.

The urgency to intervene in Liberia did not permit peacekeeping forces time to conduct joint multi-national training, prior to entering the zone of conflict. Participating forces were wedged into customized formations mapped out by the Nigerian and Ghanaian military think tanks.

Peacekeeping as well as guerilla warfare experience amongst ECOMOG forces was minimal at best. Ghana's jungle warfare specialists were mere researchers and

Trial by Rebellion

theorists with no practical experience. Senegalese troops had strong Francophone ties with the Ivory Coast and were preoccupied with a similar rebellion in its Casamance provinces. The mode of engagement in Liberia remained a thorny controversial debate among ECOWAS leaders.

Taylor's NPFL fighters thrived on organic local support. And it was far easier to create chaos than to contain it. Guerrillas had an easier objective compared to the complexity of containment. Unlike guerrillas who were willing to die challenging external interference, the peacekeeping troops were not prepared to risk death for peace.

One of the most difficult challenges ECOMOG forces faced was their inability to pacify or contain the NPFL. Taylor's NPFL rebels had far better knowledge of the operational theater and were highly motivated by narcotic drugs and the economic gains from the chaos. Guerrilla expertise required few skills. It involved willing men, gunshots, terrorized civilians, dead bodies and tailored rumors.

NPFL guerrillas comfortably outpaced peacekeeping forces, expanding the zone of conflict and effectively hitting areas devoid of troop presence. Liberia's crisis was complicated by Taylor's uncompromising ambition for power, ECOMOG's bias, and the absence of adequate conflict resolution expertise.

NPFL guerrillas routinely abused human rights. Executions, forced labor, looting and rapes were commonplace. Guerrillas especially targeted Krahn tribesmen and uncooperative civilians. Public outcry and condemnation did not stop NPFL atrocities. International aid agencies penetrated NPFL-controlled areas for relief operations, but their activities were rigorously censored to limit exposure of rebel activities to the outside world.

ECOMOG's initiative was a major political and military development lacking a decisive voice of consent over the very problem it was created to solve. ECOMOG was demonized by the NPFL as a neo military-imperialist organization, championed by sub regional military despots in support of its Liberian ally.

The Liberian civil war unfolded into a unique political challenge and exposed the existing sub-regional disunity, driven through interventionist methodologies. The international community invested its support and channeled financial resources through ECOWAS, but could not see through the curtain of dissension posing a threat to the regional body.

ECOMOG overstayed its occupation because of the many problems, an indicator of its inability to align the military operation with the desired political outcome. ECOMOG like the relentless Taylor, jointly became more of an obstacle to peace in Liberia. Sierra Leone's reception of ECOMOG gave Taylor additional reason to attack her. ECOMOG underestimated the scope of threat Taylor posed to Sierra Leone's security.

ECOMOG was obliged to safeguard Sierra Leone's security interest. In his professional capacity as former head of the armed forces and minister of defense, President Momoh could not articulate nor influence his sub-regional counterparts to recognize the strategic need to protect Sierra Leone. The geopolitical myopia was a collective blame squarely falling on the lap of sub-regional leaders present at the birth of ECOMOG.

Chapter 5

Civil war did not break out in Sierra Leone exclusively on the premise of developments in neighboring Liberia. Sierra Leone was a political magma whose explosion was overdue. A civic revolt was not dependent on time alone but a perfect opportunity. Many disgruntled elites, radical university students and graduates had reached the apex of political frustration, but could not harness the leadership and logistical support to rise against Momoh's one-party government.

The school of growing disgruntled elites stalked an occasion to express their distaste for the Momoh-led government. The Liberian crisis presented the perfect opportunity. Retired army corporal Foday Sankoh who had been falsely accused and incarcerated in the 1970s for alleged involvement in a coup plot to overthrow the APC, had enough personal reasons to mount a violent political offensive and the will of a radical manpower, but lacked the financial and strategic resources to fight the APC government. Taylor's sponsorship of Sankoh would eventually spark Sierra Leone's long fermenting political storm.

Sankoh had a strong disaffection channeled through a litany of claims against the injustices of the APC government, as a justification for his rebellion. The nation's economy was in distress. Cost of living was high and rising each year. Multi-party politics was illegal. Then there was a thread of excessive abuse of executive power over a voiceless majority. A good objective example centered around the constitutional infraction of Section (29), subsection (1), subparagraph (a) of the 1978 constitution of Sierra Leone, stating that: whenever the office of President is vacant or the holder of the office is absent from Sierra Leone or is for any reason unable to perform the functions conferred upon him by this Constitution, these functions shall be exercised by the First Vice-President, or, if there is no First Vice-President or if the First Vice-President considers that he is for any reason unable to discharge the functions of the office of President, by the Second Vice-President or such other Minister as may be appointed by the Cabinet.

In gross violation of the constitutional provision, retiring President Siaka P. Stevens handpicked Brigadier J. S. Momoh to succeed him, discarding then First Vice President S. I. Koroma as dictated by the constitution. Educated elites of the one-party legislature and the school of Sierra Leone's legal minds failed to challenge Stevens' unconstitutional power play. What was the purpose of a constitution whose rules were unquestionably defied by the President? Or better still, what was the role of the judiciary as the enforcing arm of judicial compliance?

Momoh's tribal bearing, military background, and uncompromising loyalty to Stevens' northern-dominated All People's Congress (APC), earned him the presidential nomination. A Limba by tribe with strong roots in the north, Momoh's military clout was meant to keep the constitutionally banned Sierra Leone People's Party (SLPP) forces at bay and uphold the APC legacy as a perennial power base.

Stevens was suspicious of entrusting the legacy of the APC party to Second Vice President F.M. Minah, a political offspring of the rival SLPP. Stevens' doubts made him the successful Machiavellian craftsman. He convinced the nation to believe that it needed a new direction, advertising the army Chief of Staff, Brigadier J. S. Momoh, as the best candidate to undo Sierra Leone's socio-economic stagnation.

In the ensuing single-candidate presidential election, Momoh obviously won. Symbolically, in all of Sierra Leone's twelve districts, Kailahun returned the lowest vote counts. The results were indicative of regional disaffection with the APC government. The APC was out of touch with the people of Kailahun district. Its towns and villages were separated from the capital city Freetown by a long stretch of unpaved motor roads, laced with potholes from years of neglect. Kailahun district was economically dependent on Liberia and Guinea for commerce. The bulk of its healthy cocoa and diamond proceeds ended up in Liberian and Guinean markets. The elites and local chiefs from the region were disconnected from the northern-dominated APC government. The geopolitical disconnect explains why Kailahun was the most favorable start line for the Taylor-sponsored RUF rebellion.

Momoh's subsequent presidency was accompanied by high expectations. He declared a state of "economic emergency", exposing his knowledge of the havoc his predecessor wrecked on the nation's economy. The unspoken truth was that he inherited an economy in shambles, without an immediate or long term executable strategy for its recovery. Stevens perhaps thought Momoh could use military authority to enforce public discipline as part of a recovery strategy. Sierra Leoneans invested every ounce of confidence in him and clung to prospects in his leadership.

Momoh emerged a populist with the poor and middle class majority. Flanked by seasoned political veterans, his leadership seemed like the perfect replacement for a rotten system on the verge of collapse. He was seen as a neutral, anti-corrupt, no-nonsense soldier turned politician overnight, equipped to combat corruption by enforcing public discipline.

His optimism and energy inspired a sense of conviction. His political program under a "New Order" aimed to rally the idea of "Constructive Nationalism" as a tool of collective participation to rebuild the degenerating socio-political and economic structures of his predecessor.

It was hoped that his accomplished military career would calm a nation on the verge of political explosion. He had two manifest leadership qualities, the reconciliatory and the housekeeping, mingled with a flavor of charisma. He carried the semblance of a disciplinarian, though he did not possess those traits.

Momoh's immediate challenge was to clean up the economic mess created by long years of corruption, perpetrated and jealously guarded by the same political veterans that flocked around him. His unblemished innocence and political immaturity, made him a victim of misguided counsel at the hands of those who invented the economic abyss he inherited.

Momoh was quick to recognize that leading an army with a structured hierarchy and culture of regimental discipline, differed from civil politics. His compassion, people skills and professional military leadership could not translate into good political leadership. His cabinet ministers and political advisers had years of hands-on expertise in government. His first political misstep was the composition of his cabinet. It was populated by pro-Steven loyalists and predominantly infested by a culture of corruption and unquestionable abuse of process. It reflected his helpless political infancy.

High expectations notwithstanding, Momoh's administration turned out to be a complete failure. The cost of living spiked beyond the reach of the low and middle classes. His ineffective leadership gave birth to new economic problems that had social ramifications. Diamonds that accounted for seventy percent of government revenue were indiscriminately mined and smuggled, local currency hoarded, foreign exchange squeezed out of circulation, inflation uncontainable and basic necessities including fuel, rice, and electricity ran in short supply.

Unemployment had always been high, but it soared to new heights. One in ten university graduates could barely get a job. Corruption flourished in every sector of public service. Wages were not only low but government employees worked for months without pay. Often public servants had to plead, go on strike for wages or subscribe to corruption.

Corruption became a necessary evil, destroying otherwise upright civil servants. It led to white-collar barbarism and administrative pollution of the public sector. Mismanagement of public funds, complex bureaucracies, lapses in accountability, and weak leadership nurtured boundless bubbling layers of corruption. Unpaid civil servants reconfigured public administration, transforming free public services to sources of their own informal revenue. Exemplary victims of corrupt bureaucracies were retirees compelled by administrative bureaucrats to invest half their expected earnings as collateral to speed up processing pension payouts.

Twenty-four years of one-party politics concocted a unique political cocktail which diluted the power of the executive, legislature and judiciary into inseparable branches of government. The attorney general and minister of justice were one and the same person. He was political head of the judiciary as well as a member of the executive branch of government. The role of the office compromised the independence of the judiciary. The judiciary lost its relevance to its dependence on the executive. The system had no levers for checks and balances.

Momoh's military background rendered his government immune from media criticism and effective civil political opposition. Free speech in the name of political criticism was unconstitutional and punishable without trial. Critics could only whisper their frustrations.

Trial by Rebellion

Sierra Leone's Lebanese business community evolved as another cesspool of blue-collar thuggery. Their relentless habit of bribery contributed to polluting politicians. Hand in glove with politicians, most Lebanese business owners contributed to the genesis and explosion of the culture of corruption. By 1987 when President Stevens died, the Lebanese had matured into a solidified social group, holding a major share of Sierra Leone's wealth. They spread through major cities and towns selling tobacco, radios, flour, sugar and other basic necessities, earning high dividends from every sector of commerce.

Politicians and administrative public officials turned a blind eye to the violation of administrative rules and regulations, in exchange for cash rewards from the deep pockets of rich business interests. The Lebanese earned immeasurable profits from diamond trade and freely fixed prices on consumer goods with excessive markup. Profits tapped from unregulated commerce spoonfed the capability to silence top government officials. Monetary compensation served as a powerful lobbying tool influencing legislation or inaction, to enrich rogue enterprises.

The Lebanese won government contracts, gained unfettered access to local investment capital and profited from agriculture, tourism, construction, consumer goods and fishing to the disadvantage of Sierra Leonean consumers and business interests. The towering Lebanese business moguls crumpled indigenous Sierra Leonean counterparts. In a space of twenty years following independence, the Lebanese accounted for the fastest growing block of the wealthy and powerful minority in Sierra Leone.

In 1987, Police Inspector G. M. T. KaiKai, a strong critic of Momoh's, lost his patience with the Momoh government. He attempted to overthrow President Momoh. Though unsuccessful, his was the first meaningful political opposition to Momoh's government. Vice President Minah was implicated in the plot as a co-conspirator. Evidence of Minah's involvement remains unconvincing. The trial and subsequent execution of Inspector KaiKai and Vice President Minah frightened opposition groups into obscurity.

Momoh's economic policies failed again and again. "New Order" and "Constructive Nationalism" produced no results. The nation gradually lost faith in Momoh's administration and grew silently angry and hungry, expecting a salvation in any form of political change. He lost the initiative to wrestle the deteriorating economy and honestly admitted to have "failed the nation."

Sierra Leoneans were left with no alternative to Momoh's government, nor any legal or civil avenue to effect political change. It was on the eve of such national hopelessness that Taylor co-sponsored the conception of Sankoh and his Revolutionary United Front, (RUF), representing the second wave of political revolt to Momoh's government.

Chapter 6

Taylor was an icon of incitement and inspiration to disgruntled anti-government radicals in the West African sub-region. His macro-political crusade was to engineer a successive wave of civil rebellions in West Africa, and subsequently chair the network of sub-regional guerrilla movements. He had Guineans, Sierra Leoneans and other nationals observing his model.

Whereas the Guinean government took precautionary security measures to fortify its borders with Liberia and Sierra Leone, control and contain the movement of refugees, the Sierra Leonean government adopted nonchalance.

The best of Sierra Leone's meager armament, anti-personnel carriers and troops had already been deployed in Liberia as part of the ECOMOG intervention force. With little reserve forces and no contingency plan to handle uncertainties, military authorities left the home front with a skeleton force ill prepared to deal with looming threat to its national security.

To measure the level of ill preparedness of the national army, one need look no further than the incident that unfolded in Bomaru on March 14, 1991. The unregulated border trade of loots from Liberia sparked an altercation between Sierra Leone army officers and

NPFL fighters over seizure of a looted car. The misunderstanding sparked an armed brawl, costing the lives of two army officers, the very first Sierra Leonean army casualties.

The incident was a test case designed by Taylor's war council, to gauge Sierra Leone's army's state of readiness to respond to external threats. Less than a month after the Bomaru fracas, Sankoh went public over the British Broadcasting Corporation's "Focus on Africa," challenging President Momoh to reinstate multi-party politics within ninety days or be ousted. Theoretically, reform modalities to amend the constitution to legalize multi-party politics was in progress, though the lethargic pace of the process made it highly suspect.

Several clashes had already been reported between government forces and the combined NPFL- RUF guerillas prior to the expiration of the ultimatum. The troubling question that remains unanswered to this day is this: Where was Sankoh at the time of the proclamation of his ultimatum and how did the British press reach him? Did Sankoh call the British media, or was it the other way around? Who were the facilitators pioneering the communication?

Sankoh's ninety-day ultimatum was aired via BBC's infrastructure using cellular equipment, but was Sankoh in Taylor's headquarters in Gbanga or on the Sierra Leone border? The proof of Taylor's direct involvement to destabilize Sierra Leone can be traced to the communication between the BBC and its dealings with the rebels.

Trial by Rebellion

Sankoh's ultimatum was a crafty instrument of pressure. Sankoh suspected the APC was neither prepared to hasten the process of pluralism, nor felt threatened to cave in to his demands. The Revolutionary United Front (RUF), in concert with drugged NPFL guerrillas, easily took control of the key commercial towns of Buedu, Koindu, Bunumbu, and Kailahun without resistance from a country that claimed to have an army.

Like a virus, they effortlessly populated border towns east and south of Sierra Leone, including Sulima, Zimmi, Dia, Normo Farma, Yenga, Jojoima, Fairo, and Bunumbu, penetrated inland toward major district headquarter towns. Kailahun and Pujehun districts were swiftly swallowed, subjecting its residents to the dictates of rebel administration.

The RUF made Buedu its headquarters for strategic reasons. It was the crossing point to either Guinea or Liberia. RUF's administration was a hierarchy of one supreme leader and a conglomerate of secondary leaders. Sub-leaders included local chiefs and rebel commanders. Laws were promulgated and enforced at the dictates of Foday Sankoh, the supreme leader.

It is hard to conceive whether Momoh's concession to Sankoh's terms within the ninety-day timeframe would have deterred the joint Taylor–Sankoh scheme to invade Sierra Leone. Sankoh had already established a base of operations in Buedu on the Sierra Leone-Liberia border, well ahead of the completion of the ninety-day ultimatum. Momoh's negation of the ultimatum awarded Sankoh the justification to launch his political rebellion.

Sankoh indirectly incited Sierra Leoneans, including opposition leaders to support or join him in rising against the APC government. His conviction was deeply rooted in the perceived frustration over appalling national economic conditions.

Appealing as the idea of overthrowing the APC may have been, the movement did not attract its expected nationwide appeal, partly because of the existing fear of Momoh's one-party government and partly because of the horrific events in neighboring Liberia that were cascaded in the news. Taylor's model of violence as a tool for political change was unpopular in Sierra Leone.

The unpopularity of violence not withstanding, the RUF gained early successes along border towns. The successes stemmed from the attractive theme of his political message. Sankoh preyed on the political sentiments of the Mende tribal groups dominant in the east and south. They were wholly inclined to see an end to APC rule or the return of multi-party politics, which would pave the way for the emergence of the Sierra Leone People's Party (SLPP).

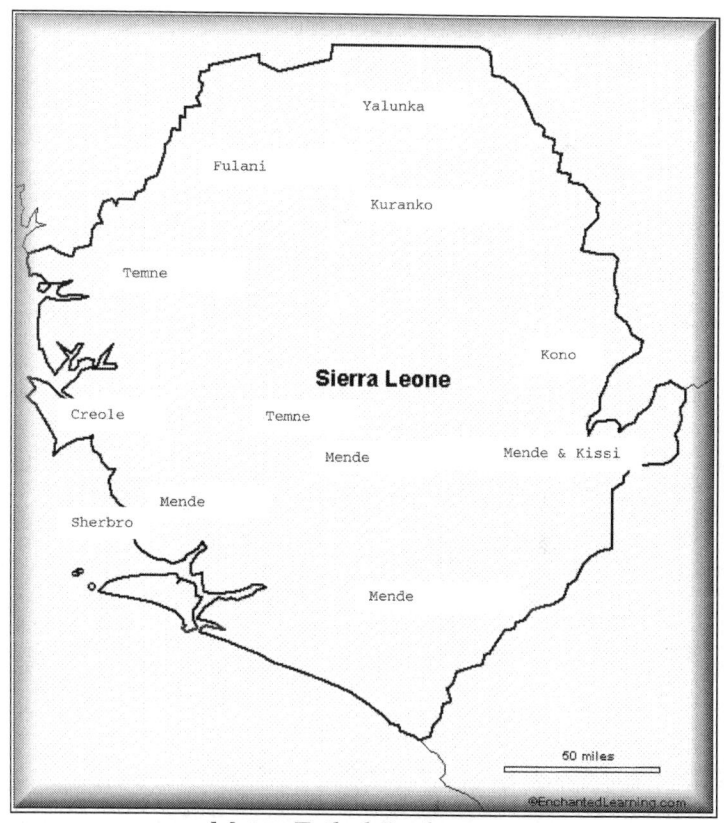

Major Tribal Settlements

Sankoh's rebellious uprising awakened political nostalgia, resurrecting images of the Sierra Leone Peoples Party (SLPP), economic prosperity, and political inclusion. Largely a SLPP support base, politically volatile and frustrated farmers, local elites, youths, and traditional leaders in the southeast, the majority of who were Mendes and Kissis, were attracted to the rebellion.

In addition to the receptiveness of its local population, the southeast was economically lucrative and geographically congenial for guerrilla warfare. The aged forestry, unpaved secondary roads, network of footpaths, and ample sources of food offered rebels a haven for guerrilla operations.

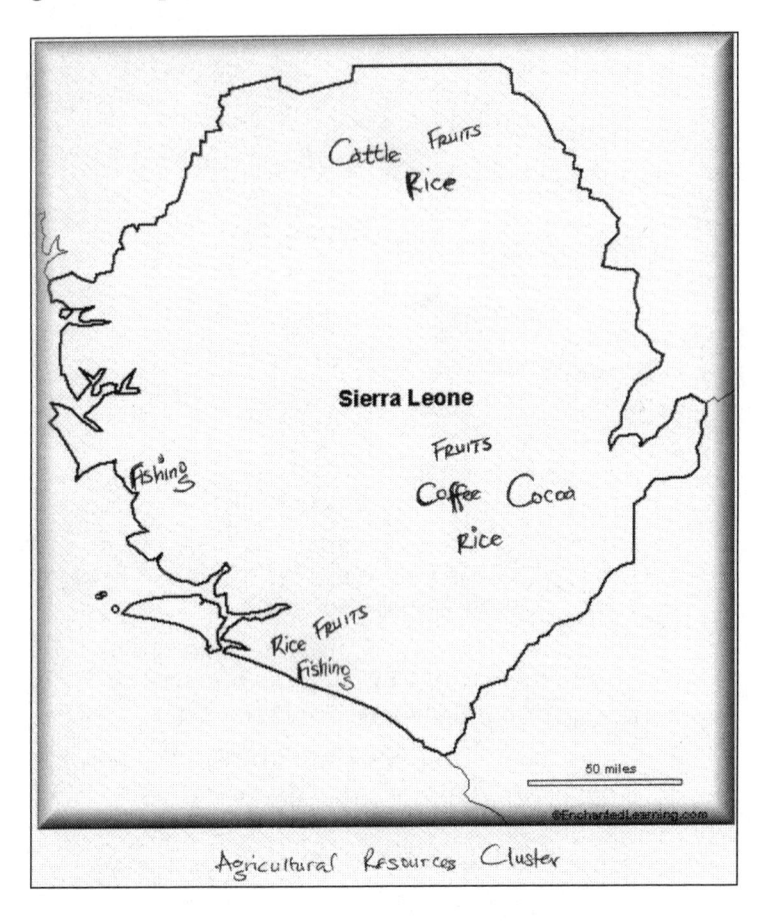

Agricultural Resources Cluster

Trial by Rebellion

The movement milked on cash crops, mainly coffee, cocoa, timber, and kimberlite diamond deposits in the south and east to fund its operations. Like Liberia, the chaos in Sierra Leone presented an opportunity worth more economic than political gains.

Rebels attacked innocent, defenseless civilians along the border towns, killed unwilling supporters, disloyal conscripts and a handful of known pro-APC supporters in the east and south. In the guise of a liberation struggle to free the masses from a corrupt one-party government, the majority of the innocent masses ironically became prime victims of the violence.

Poorly equipped and tactically ill prepared, the army leadership found itself scrambling to put up a last-minute defense. The army plotted battle plans and wrote operation orders using outdated maps. Real time changes in the landscape and footpaths used by the RUF were not reflected on maps. Guerrilla advances were so fast and successful, almost all initial defenses put up by the army failed.

The RUF's primary preoccupation was the capture and occupation or demolition of the Daru Barracks. Positioned on top of a hill overlooking the town of Daru and the Moa River, the barracks was more than a military installation.

The capture of the barracks was key to the RUF's momentum and so was its retention by the army. Daru barracks held a tactical psychological value to both the RUF and the army defending it. It was home to soldiers and their families. It was also a symbol of pride to the army. Its capitulation would have been a psychological springboard to RUF's momentum and total annihilation of the army. The army, like Sankoh, knew that priceless fact and focused a lot of energy and resources to it.

A military facility closest to the Liberian border, the barracks housed tons of logistical supplies, had training facilities and was home to many of Sankoh's former army colleagues. Disoriented by the NPFL and RUF's multi-pronged assaults along the border, troops withdrew to the barracks.

To capture the barracks from its occupants, the joint NPFL-RUF rebels flanked all inbound and outbound roads leading to the barracks with diabolic, mile-long, staggered ambushes. Simultaneously, they engaged the troops in a round-the-clock attack to force a depletion of the ammunition stock held in the fort. The ambush was meant to starve off any form of troop reinforcements or ammunition replenishment.

The rebels attacked the barracks from every flank but met unyielding resistance. The death toll was extremely high on both sides. Taylor's NPFL fighters were later distinguished from RUF fighters by identity cards bearing NPFL logos found on those killed in action. The army also lost many of its brave men. Many more sustained serious physical and psychological injuries that would later impact the nation's political transposition.

Lieutenant V. E. M. Strasser (who later became the Head of State and chairman of the National Provisional Ruling Council in 1992), Lieutenant Julius Maada Bio, Lieutenant Charles Bayoh, Lieutenant Kumba Kambo, Private Idrissa Kamara, Private Tom S. Nyuma (all of who later became key officers of the NPRC governing council), and the late Lieutenant Teddy Koroma were among the few junior officers who defended RUF's assault on the Daru barracks. A point worth noting was the absence of a defense strategy. The army's defense of Daru was achieved by unsubmissive willpower to retain the ego of an institutional bastion and its occupying associates.

Daru's fall to the RUF would have provided Sankoh a major psychological edge over the army. Control of the Daru Garrison by the RUF could have emboldened the RUF's resolve. Without a major staging area, the army may have lost total control of the east and south to Sankoh much more quickly.

The barracks would have provided the RUF an operational step-up headquarters. Total control of the eastern provinces would have been easily accomplished by psychological rather than military means. The army held its ground.

Unable to capture the Daru barracks from the army, Sankoh resorted to a psychological approach. Among other things, he orchestrated unfounded rumors, claiming the commanding officer of the Daru garrison, Lieutenant Colonel L. M. S. Turay was a sympathizer of the RUF. The unsubstantiated and uncontested misinformation impacted the morale of troops. The garrison commander became the RUF's first victim of propaganda attacks. Lieutenant Colonel Turay was immediately recalled from the front and placed under an intelligence watch, robbing him of years of deserved reputation.

One of the major tactical flaws that militated against the army leadership's ability to contain the NPFL-RUF rebels was the application of conventional tactics to an unconventional warfare. Senior officers planned battles and wrote orders in the comfort of their offices, miles away from the enemy, using bits and pieces of unreliable intelligence data. As a result, the army struggled to recover and hold large portions of ground from RUF occupation. Defense of captured grounds consumed the army's manpower. The RUF on their part, continuously pursued the offensive mode overstretching the army's manpower.

Junior officers were pushed to the forward edge of the front to execute flaw-ridden battle plans that always failed. Arms, ammunitions and other logistical items were still rationed out at the expense of the soldiers who put their lives in harm's way.

Sierra Leoneans initially viewed the war as an incursion from Liberia, but Sankoh's managerial role localized the war, shaping his message as a fight against a failed government. As much as the Sierra Leone war was spoonfed by Taylor to avenge Momoh's refusal to support his cause, it was also partly a domestic bread and butter conflict. Sankoh thought his impoverished colleagues in the army would mutiny and allow him an easy ride to the seat of power.

Chapter 7

The RUF's reputation for indiscriminate killings forced residents within close proximity to the south and eastern fronts, to abandon towns and villages long before the rebels arrived. Desertion played into the hands of RUF's psychology of chaos.

The RUF portrayed the voluntary desertion of villages and towns as part of its strategy and ability to outrun government's every effort to contain the chaos. It created the impression that the RUF was taking the fight to the army.

In the east, for example, the combined RUF and NPFL guerrillas penetrated the army's line of defense by tactical infiltration through the Mano River Bridge on the border with Liberia to Joru junction, barely eighteen miles to Kenema town.

Outmaneuvered by the RUF's multi-pronged advances, the army leadership finally realized that the national recall of retired and dismissed soldiers alone was not enough manpower to contain the RUF. The Special Security Division, (SSD), of the police was also committed to combat.

After several months of little progress, the army leadership embarked on a massive recruitment drive. For the first time, the army leadership removed patronage, tribal affiliation, and nepotism from its recruitment policy. Young unemployed men flocked the national call to military service, partly as an expression of patriotism and partly as a means to an economic end.

The flood of unemployed youths provided the manpower required to stall the RUF's speedy advances. Wartime trainees usually make good combatants because they train with a mindset on war. Recruits were groomed purely to operate rifles, shot to kill, conventional combat maneuvers and thrown into the field to fight.

Regimental soldiering was shelved as a post-war project. The new recruits were hastily weaved into various battalions. Tiger battalion used the Daru barracks as its headquarters, with the rebel stronghold of Kailahun as its axis of advance. Scorpion battalion had its headquarters in Koribundo, outside Bo Town, with Pujehun and Sulima as its objective. Cobra battalion had its headquarters in Kenema Town with the Mano River Bridge on the border with Liberia as its objective.

The army immediately launched an all out offensive on all three fronts, to push the RUF back to the border villages. ULIMO detachments operating from the Sierra Leonean border, contributed to recapture Neyama Jawei, Ngolahun Tunkia, Zimmi, Gufor, on to the Mano River bridge. ULIMO forces also supported Scorpion battalion to recapture Potoru and Pujehun.

Trial by Rebellion

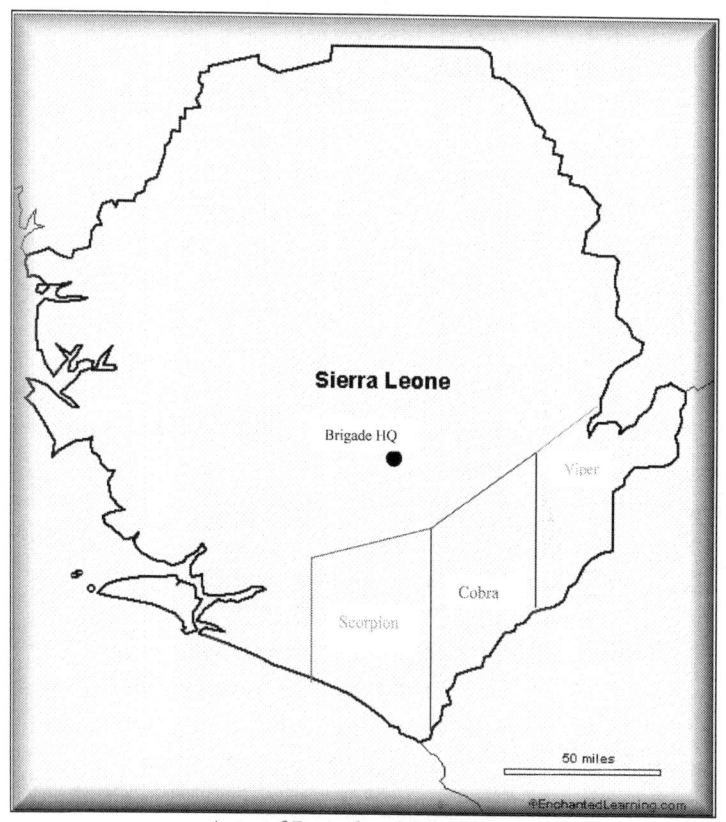

Axis of Battalion Operation

Young officers quickly perfected and planned around RUF's hit and run guerillas tactics and developed methods of dealing with guerrillas. Troops started hosting conversations with rebels in the heat of combat to establish a sense of strength, confidence and control.

The enthusiasm of young officers and their men froze RUF's momentum. Government troops quickly regained footholds in strategic villages on the border whose occupation by the RUF, posed a threat to major towns. The RUF had a problem with the army's firepower and avoided it as best as possible.

The RUF recognized the army's reliance on vehicular mobility to re-supply troops with rations and ammunition. Rather than waste armament and manpower in firefights, they shifted tactics, resorting to covert ambushes on convoys along bad roads.

With the RUF tentatively contained to the villages along the Liberian border, the army leadership planned a major offensive targeted at regaining the RUF strongholds in Kailahun. Then General Staff Officer of training and foot runner of the military leadership, Major Kelly Conteh spearheaded the creation of a new battalion.

Populated by a composition of war-weary Sierra Leonean soldiers returning from the ECOMOG front in Liberia, new recruits from training school and select seasoned fighters from Scorpion, Tiger, and Cobra battalions, the new battalion was headed by Lieutenant Colonel Anderson.

The General Staff officer of policy and planning since the inception of the Sankoh-led war, Anderson was unqualified for the extraordinary task. The appointment of a senior infantry officer with no exposure to guerilla warfare to capture the RUF's strongest tactical positions in Kailahun was an irresponsible and miscalculated decision.

Gladio battalion's mission was to advance toward Kuiva, Bomaru, Senga, Bunumbu, and Pendembu

Trial by Rebellion

through Nyandehun Junction simultaneously. Its operation orders were drawn on a sketchy intelligence on the RUF. The operation was charged with an excessive inventory of manpower directly from training school and operation orders written by staff officers who had never fired a shot since the inception of the war.

The battle plan was such a fine imaginative phantom on paper. Gladio's mission was to dislocate the central cord of the RUF movement by an attack, recapture, and defense all at once. An operation of such vital importance was planned and coordinated without due consideration of how lethal the RUF could be in their zone of dominance. Uncertainties were not forecasted nor were contingency plans conceived.

The young battalion had stockpiles of arms, ammunitions, communications equipments and the fullest support of the army headquarters. Gladio battalion was additionally backed by a Crack Unit: a platoon of high powered support weapons with 82-millimeter mortars, twin-barreled anti-aircraft gun, mounted on ten-wheel trucks and artillery fire support on call from the Guinean troops deployed in Daru. The battalion's firepower was supposed to be overwhelming.

The missing component was a realistic battle plan, an experienced commander, and solid intelligence on the strength, movement and activities of the enemy in their area of tactical superiority. In contrast to the army, the RUF operated on a low-budget communication and intelligence infrastructure that was so efficient, it kept the ragtag rebel group one step ahead of the army.

The RUF invested much of its meager resources to collect solid intelligence. The group relied on up-to-date human intelligence provided by the local residents. RUF spies disguised as civilians took bold initiatives to infiltrate army deployments to assess weapons capabilities, headcount, and even such minor details as troop habits.

A trained communication technician, Sankoh also utilized previous training and experience in military communications to monitor the army's radio frequency, with similar radio equipment and discreet call signs used by the army. Morse codes were deciphered and radio conversations intercepted, giving the RUF control of firsthand information on the movement of troops and supplies.

The majority of government troop and ammunition transportation was conducted in broad daylight without secrecy. Public display of troop activities may have been vital to harness public support and garner confidence, but it was tactically unprofessional.

The show of force heading to the frontline proved a double-edged sword. It raised a lot of expectations amongst the civilian population. The unclassified movement of troops and ammunition quickly echoed in Sankoh's camp. It also supplied the RUF vital information of a major offensive, giving the RUF lead time to plan the demise of the battalion. Several of these tactical loopholes plagued Gladio battalion's plan of attack on the RUF's strongest position.

Chapter 8

Lieutenant Colonel Daniel K. Anderson, marshaled his battalion in the strategic town of Nyeyama Jawei, as a step up to dislodge the RUF from its headquarters in Kailahun district. Nyeyama was at a crossroads between the Kenema and Kailahun districts. Twenty- nine miles from Kenema, Nyeyama was formerly a rebel stronghold and training camp. It was recaptured by Cobra battalion personnel and defended by three platoons for its tactical value.

Phase one of Gladio battalion's advance was a tactical leap of troops and supplies from Nyeyama to Nyadehun Junction. The leap was the principal flaw of the operation. The mobilization of a huge inventory of men and weapons into a very tiny, non -tactical, unprotected village lay outside rational battle reasoning.

Before heading out to the operational start line, the battalion commander also had a responsibility to address his men in person about the pending mission. The content of his address should have been focused on the psychological preparation of his men, a motivational trigger if you will, to instill anger and rage at the enemy they were about to confront. It never happened. Anderson brought army headquarters' culture of distancing themselves from the rest of the troops. He spent his time in seclusion, issuing conventional orders to subordinate commanders by the book. Experienced troops detached from other battalions relied on spirited and face to face interaction with every level of command. The bulk of experienced troops felt disconnected and unmotivated by the structured approach adopted by the commander. New graduates from the military academy had no time to bond with experienced fighters in the battalion. These minute nuances led to an organic bottleneck unforeseen by the battalion commander.

Gladio Battalion thinned out of Nyeyama, leaving behind an eerie silence filled with anticipation, suspense and hope. That night was quiet and foggy, with clouds clustered in odd shapes against a moonless sky. The next morning was unusually tense with an air of expectation.

Early that following afternoon, the continuous thump of mortar bombs and exploding rocket-propelled grenades echoing through the forest void sounded unusually closer to Nyeyama. It was indicative of Gladio's contact with the RUF. The explosive blasts lasted all that early afternoon, with sustained small arms fire in the background.

Gladio battalion's radio operators were on the radio relaying the battle situation report. The stress of their voices was worrying. Knowing the many tricks of the guerrillas, there was a feeling the battalion had been cut off from the rear.

Late that afternoon, all operations areas lost radio contact with Gladio battalion. The radio silence was an operational omen. Nyeyama was on alert for possible RUF attack. Pockets of soldiers began surfacing in Nyeyama that afternoon, relaying how the operation had gone amok. The passing hours brought in withdrawing Gladio soldiers from nearby bushes in every direction, with stories of a poorly executed battle plan.

The whereabouts of the battalion commander and his deputy remained unknown at the time. Whether alive, dead, captured, or on the run, one thing was clear: Gladio battalion had lost central command. Junior officers took command of their platoons into withdrawal mode.

Gladio battalion's dismemberment exposed the depth of an incapable military leadership and the extent of its inefficiency to plan prematurely without much analytic depth. It was one of the worst military operations and strategic losses the army incurred to the RUF. In comparison to the nation's army commander, Sankoh's rebel commander proved to be both brave and more adept tactical planner.

The RUF capitalized on solid intelligence data effectively utilized to plan the attack of an entire battalion clustered in a village with less than six houses and no trenches. The RUF launched a surprise attack on Gladio battalion in Nyandehun junction, focusing its firepower on logistical supplies loaded in trucks in plain sight. The unexpected attack robbed the battalion of all initiative, as it prepared for its next leap to Kuiva.

With no trenches, few houses to provide cover from incoming fire and no effective command and control, the battalion was outgunned in Nyandehun Junction. Gladio officers and men were left to operate in isolation, abandoning equipment, arms and ammunition.

Given the situation, the safest option to minimize casualties was a hasty withdrawal. Junior officers engaged in the operations were left angry and disappointed by the poor planning that led to a flawed execution of the battle plan. They could not contain their anger at the reckless endangerment of their lives.

The fall of Gladio accentuated the striking incompetence of senior officers. The tactical prowess and mystique of President Momoh's trusted senior officers was lost in the dusty heap of Gladio battalion's disintegration.

The weeks following the fall of Gladio saw soldiers missing in action surface in Daru and Nyeyama, recounting harrowing tales of their survival in the jungle. The fall of Gladio battalion impacted both the RUF and the army. The army lost costly resources and motivation.

With stockpiles of arms and ammunition captured from the army, the RUF seized the initiative to launch new offensives. This exemplifies the strings of poor decisions made by the military leadership that rendered Sankoh a force to reckon with.

Chapter 9

Following the demise of Gladio battalion, the RUF realized the tactical threat the troops occupying Nyeyama posed to its strongholds. Nyeyama served as a strategic bypass route to RUF's positions in Kailahun. Of twenty-three attacks on Nyeyama, sixteen were launched immediately after the fall of Gladio.

The RUF was relentless in the use of its offensive strategy, creating the illusion that the RUF had a larger fighting force. Military positions in the east and south were sometimes attacked simultaneously, in addition to ambushes that always netted huge military casualties.

The RUF sometimes pitched camp a few miles away from army positions, drumming through the night to create the illusion of a fearless motivated force. Sometimes rebel commanders were heard yelling "one thousand RUF advance" during attacks. They also used simulators, which echoed like heavy machine guns, or fired small arms through large drums giving off sounds like high powered support weapons.

Occasionally, children, women and feeble old men were coerced to scout or spy, to collect any amount of information they could. The RUF had one remarkable quality—the flexibility to utilize espionage teams disguised as civilians escaping RUF camps. RUF spies caught by government troops withheld detailed information on RUF locations and activities during interrogative questioning, on the premise that giving up classified information on RUF activities would not exonerate them from the belief that execution awaits them at the hands of government troops.

The impregnable fronts manned by the raw zest of youthful, motivated and energetic young officers with loyal troops hardly capitulated to the persistence of RUF offensives. One key factor accounting for the stout defenses was based on mathematical estimation mixed with bravery. Junior commanders estimated that the average RUF combatant carried no more than four loaded ammunition magazines, containing 24 rounds of 7.62 ammunition. Unaccustomed to firing in automatic mode, it was deduced that out of a total of 96 shots, 72 would be expended in action and 24 reserved for withdrawal.

In major offensives, they carried more ammunitions and paired up in teams of twos, one gunner with an assistant reloading empty magazines and acting as a secondary watch person. On occasion, they took breaks between attacks to rest, reload, re-strategize, or swap fighting teams. The RUF also had a habit of announcing their presence before an attack. That gave army mortar specialists time to gauge their distance. The position of attacking RUF rebels was pounded with mortar bombs to soften or throw their attack formation off balance. Surprisingly, no amount of mortar fire inhibited RUF attacks.

Trial by Rebellion

The unshakeable bond between junior officers and troops on one hand and that between troops and local civilians on the other, added itself to strategies used to fend off the RUF. Soldiers showed an uncompromising loyalty to their immediate junior commanders.

The origin of such undying loyalty hailed from the junior commanders making themselves accessible and approachable. Lines of communication were open for exchanging ideas. Junior commanders also showed a strong sense of concern for troop welfare—the true mark of wartime leadership.

Local civilian support also provided a unique value to troops. Locals supplied frontline troops with meat, palm oil, fruits and other vital foodstuffs to supplement inadequate combat rations—one cup of uncooked rice, two dried fish and a cup of raw peanuts.

Locals helped brush bushy roads, cooked for troops and performed sentry night watch. In return, combat medics offered civilians free medical treatment. Civilians also traveled aboard military vehicles with goods to the market at no expense. Often, when RUF guerrillas threatened the freedom of civilian movement to farms in search of food, government soldiers shared combat rations with locals until threats were curtailed.

In contrast to the army, the RUF maintained a different style of discipline within its organization in relation to civilians. The relationship between rebels and locals was based on strict controls, censorship, limited freedom of movement and forced labor. Rebel commanders did not compromise with their fighters either.

Rebel commanders laid greater emphasis on coerced loyalty, reward and brutal punishment. Rebel commanders led with a fist of brutality, discouraged defection by brainwashing conscripts and supporters to believe, that should they surrender to government forces, they would be executed by firing squads.

The strategy deterred unwilling conscripts from opting out of the RUF organization. Attempts to escape RUF camps were treated as high treason and punishable by execution. Would-be defectors were trapped between the RUF's brainwashing strategies and the Sierra Leone Army's ineffective propaganda machinery.

Chapter 10

The most sophisticated of RUF attacks on Nyeyama was launched unexpectedly one hot February afternoon. Dogs in the village had been barking all morning, signaling suspicious activities. That afternoon, troops spotted plumes of smoke a mile away from Nyeyama. It was common for guerrillas to announce their presence by wrecking havoc and then retreating, leaving troops in an intense state of alert.

There was some concern for brave civilians who had ventured into the woods to fetch food that morning. A handful of them returned shaken and out of breath, with news that the RUF guerrillas had pitched camp half a mile way from Nyeyama. The commander of the RUF squad, they exclaimed, intended to capture and cut off the heads of the officers and render Nyeyama uninhabitable. The troops immediately occupied trenches. Section commanders made for the tactical headquarters for ammunition replenishment.

Two sections of sixteen men armed with heavy support weapons took a foot patrol in the direction of the billowing smoke. Except for houses torched and left to burn in the unoccupied village, the patrol yielded no confrontation. Another village half a mile to the rear of Nyeyama with moderate civilian population had been simultaneously attacked and set ablaze. Massive tree trunks were felled across the roads to stall reinforcements bound for Nyeyama. Young men and women were abducted and older civilians shot or left to escape. Another section was mobilized to confront the rebels, but arrived a little too late. The rebels were long gone, leaving behind their signature of torched houses, dead bodies and an eerie silence.

The brief chaos had been a well crafted decoy. RUF snipers had been positioning themselves in treetops to prepare for an all out assault on Nyeyama. The rest of the day rolled over quietly into a tense night. At the crack of dawn, two rocket-propelled grenades zoomed directly over the tactical headquarters, one of them tearing the roof of the local courthouse. A barrage of small arms fire rattled from all directions.

The trajectory of shots digging into the ground eventually gave away the position of snipers. Three soldiers in a trench had taken hits. After half an hour of incoming fire, rebels, mostly teens, could be seen cautiously emerging from the foggy mist of the forest. Adults could be heard in the background yelling, *"Advance!"*

With the motorable road leading into Nyeyama rendered impenetrable by tree trunks felled across the road, some level of tactical restraint was necessary to manage the ammunition stock. Replenishment and troop reinforcement could not be guaranteed. The roads would be laced with ambushes.

Trial by Rebellion

Nyeyama's defense narrowed down to two options: regulation of shots at rebels in plain sight or unleashing overwhelming firepower to inflict massive casualties, hoping it could deflate their morale and influence a withdrawal. Risky as it was, the latter was chosen. The danger was an absence of a contingency plan, should the plan fail.

Troops on the east flank with better visibility of RUF fighters eventually initiated the firefight. Like a blazing inferno, all other flanks joined in unleashing the full content of firepower. The twin barrel anti-aircraft machine gun proved effective for the snipers. Snipers were frightening by the roaring sound of its tracer rounds emitting fire in its flight and slicing off huge tree branches. They could be spotted in the distance dropping off trees and screaming in anguish.

After the all-out volley of fire that lasted roughly 2,222 seconds, a brief observatory silence ensued. Against the background of the ceasefire, one could hear crying, moaning and screaming piercing the momentary relief. By sundown, the guerrillas launched fresh attacks. The renewed attack was a ploy to deter troops from pursuing them as they picked up the wounded and the dead for withdrawal.

As a fundamental psychology of guerrilla warfare, rebels hardly ever left their casualties behind. The strategy was meant to demoralize soldiers after an attack. Evidence of dead rebels were either dragged away or concealed, undercutting the army's ability to claim successes. It was meant to give soldiers the perception of the invincibility of the rebels from bullets. In the heat of the battle that day, the strategy failed. RUF guerrillas tripped booby traps made of clustered pineapple grenades deployed as additional defenses in all likely approaches. The indiscriminate explosions from booby traps further destabilized their withdrawal. A search of the perimeter the next day revealed a high rate of rebel casualty. A few dead bodies were tucked under tree branches and piles of dead leaves, but most lay where they had been shot. Trails of blood, weapons, empty ammunition pouches, shoes, and drums littered the woods.

After thrashing RUF's manpower, the probability of a rematch was high. What was uncertain was when and with what tricks. The next brazen attack to reclaim Nyeyama was launched at night. It was extremely rare for the RUF to attack at night. It failed prematurely. The RUF finally abandoned Nyeyama to relative quiet.

Chapter 11

During the brief periods of downtime from combat action with RUF rebels, radical junior officers began to weigh the possibility and strategy to overthrow President Momoh. It was supposed to be spontaneous and may have occurred before April 28, 1992. The controversial death of Captain Ben Hirsch, one of the masterminds of the plan, delayed the execution of the coup.

A popular young officer, Captain Ben Hirsh was an excellent field operations officer, crafty planner and motivator, who attracted a large troop following. He was more popular than his battalion commander. He co-invented the idea of commandeering government vehicles exclusively for operational use in the battle front. It was the earliest sign of a challenge to the government's lack of response to the logistical needs of frontline troops.

His sudden death in a questionable ambush whilst mobilizing troops for an RUF offensive, sent a cold chill through the spine of many young officers. The coup planners felt the APC government had him assassinated.

Captain Valentine Strasser, who later became Head of State and Chairman of the ruling military government, along with Lieutenant Kumba Kambo, who became Undersecretary of Defense, both nursed unforgettable grievances regarding the government's neglect of frontline troops. Lieutenant Kambo had used his wages and family help to tend his medical condition, knowing the army did not care about the likes of him and others. While on medical leave, he shared his frustrations with Captain Strasser and many other patients in the military hospital.

The painful deaths of a notable colleague, Lieutenant Massa Koroma, (aka, Teddy), Captain Ben Hirsh, and many soldiers angered the young officers. The painful losses reminded the radical young officers of the sadistic propensity of the entire army leadership, including the government they served.

Lieutenant Massa Koroma had sustained a severe gaping wound to his lower abdomen, rupturing his organs, during RUF's initial assault on the Daru barracks in 1991. He was one of the oldest patients in a military hospital starved of medical resources. Lieutenant Koroma held to life through a feeding tube, available medical attention and courageous nurses. He was a patriotic hero whose life could have been saved with better medical attention. He eventually died and was whisked to the military grave, buried and forgotten.

In contrast to soldiers in combat, politicians had the luxury of excellent medical treatment at home and abroad. The military hospital continued to host increasing fatalities that shocked military families. In all those painful moments, not a single politician or the senior military leadership ever spent time with the men at the overcrowded hospital. Military funerals were so overwhelming, some had to be conducted quietly in the front. Some families never got to see their fathers, brothers, uncles, sons, and daughters and instead got the sad news that their relatives were killed in action.

Following his discharge from the hospital, Captain Strasser, who himself had sustained a shrapnel injury to his leg, along with Lieutenant Kambo, Charles Bayoh and Second Lieutenant Mondeh, in concert with other ranks, decided to revive the plan to topple Momoh's government. For these officers it was time for a change. Captain Julius Maada Bio assumed the role and command of the late Captain Ben Hirsh in Segbwema, a few miles from the Daru barracks. He became the tactical centerpoint of contact for the execution of the coup plot.

He took charge of selectively recruiting likeminded young officers and troops and smuggling ammunition in his tactical headquarter, referred to as the U*nder Cellar.* It was the non-tactical rallying point where most young officers along the Daru axis met to wind down from the frontline.

There were two independent plots to overthrow President Momoh. The first, schemed by young officers along the Daru axis, originated from the Ben Hirsch plan. The plotters were cautiously methodical. The timing, long planning and level of detail was geared toward a perfect execution, knowing that a failure would have had fatal consequences.

Second Lieutenants Nyuma and Sandy, both platoon commanders operating from Nyeyama were the exclusive architects of the second plot. The Nyeyama plan differed from Daru's based on the proposed method of execution. Lieutenants Nyuma and Sandy had this illusion that the Cobra battalion commander, Lieutenant Colonel Yahayh Kanu, had been giving out motivational clues and innuendoes to overthrow the APC government.

Nyuma and Sandy's plan was to identify officers, recruit, rally, brief and mobilize the required forces to Freetown at short notice. The short timespan was to avoid leaks and to achieve the element of surprise. Captain S. A. J. Musa, Second Lieutenants Nyuma and Sandy eventually consolidated the Daru and Kenema plans into a whole.

Second Lieutenant Nyuma who later became secretary of state of the Eastern Province before his appointment as Undersecretary of defense, grew up in an era of radical anti-APC political activism on the Fourah Bay College campus, where his father worked.

He witnessed firsthand the riots of radical University students and later became a fanatic convert of the Pan African organization (PANAFU). He also passionately embraced the Green Book movement, its doctrines anchored in radical political revolutionary thoughts aimed at uprooting the vestiges of narrowing opportunity for younger Africans.

Second Lieutenant Nyuma's revolutionary ambition also fed on military political literature of renowned African military leaders like General Afrifa of Ghana, Thomas Sankara of Burkina Faso, Ghadafi in Libya, Generals Buhari and Babaginda of Nigeria. He studied these men with a passion and memorized extracts of their speeches. He knew in microscopic detail how these soldiers marched to power. Like the late Ben Hirsch, he was extremely popular and attracted a large troop following.

Nyuma's principal accomplice, Second Lieutenant Shar Samuel Sandy, (aka "Blood"), claimed his radical molding in secondary school. A fearless young man of few words, he attended St. Edwards Secondary School in Freetown. Then he developed a passion for the army, with a strong desire to accomplish something for which he would be remembered. Lieutenant Sandy had a habit of collecting and memorizing quotes, justifying why it was necessary to overthrow any government that failed to meet the needs of its people.

His favorite quote read, "… the preponderance of dwindling economic prospects in a nation with immeasurable wealth, need not allow its leaders to prevail without questioning the object of their authority. It is therefore a moral duty, a calling to her citizens to undo a failing leadership by legal or other means as it sees fit."

The young radical officers had a common creed—that government had a social contract to its people, and more importantly, its soldiers in combat. They felt that politicians deserved a civic education regarding their responsibilities and the value of the equally precious lives of patriotic soldiers.

The motivation to overthrow the APC government was rooted in the belief that senior officers in Freetown were incompetent cowards unfit to lead men in war. They had neither combat experience nor the guts to wrestle with the RUF or young frontline officers in a firefight. On a philosophical level, the coup plotters felt it was more heroic to die standing up to a failed government than to die fighting an organization of ragtag guerrillas, whose liberation struggle was making little headway.

The political belief was that the overthrow of the APC would pacify Sankoh and subsequently end the civil conflict. It had become extremely boring to fight a war with no end in sight. The war, it was believed, had a political, not a military solution. The military campaign was therefore unnecessary and could only end by terminating the reign of the APC government.

By its action and inaction, the sacrifice of a soldier's life to the reigning APC government was reduced to an insignificant value. Soldiers no longer felt it was worth risking death as an expression of patriotism in a mismanaged war. Absence without leave, (AWOL), from the frontline became a new problem. Unmotivated, soldiers abandoned frontlines, discarded their rifles and uniforms, and even refused to collect their meager salaries.

Unsubstantiated and unchallenged rumors of RUF sympathizers in the higher echelon of the army also aggravated the depletion of troops from the front.

Trial by Rebellion

The military police mounted checkpoints along highways leading to all major cities and conducted large-scale arrests of combatants, breeding the most bitter hate for senior military and political leadership. Troop presence in Freetown was drained down to almost nil.

The diversion of troops outside Freetown set the stage for the coup planners, who were cognizant of the opportunities presented by the prevailing morale problem in the army. They also sensed the manifest political unpopularity of Momoh's government.

Chapter 12

The final countdown to Momoh's reign began on the afternoon of April 28, 1992, in Kenema. Commanding Officer of Cobra battalion, Lieutenant Colonel Yahya Kanu and Brigade Commander, Colonel Turay, traveled to Freetown early that afternoon to attend a staff and command meeting at the army Headquarters.

Lieutenant Colonel Kanu was to relinquish command of Cobra battalion to assume command of Sierra Leone's ECOMOG contingent in Liberia. Coup plotters saw the development as the perfect opportunity to strike Freetown. The assumption was that Kanu would be disgruntled at his redeployment to Monrovia and would likely defect to support a coup involving young officers.

In its planning and execution, the coup was a blueprint of the overthrow of Ghana's late President Kwame Nkrumah. After his education in the United States of America, Nkrumah returned to Ghana to become President. He developed a religious devotion to the ideals of communist policy of state ownership and sharing of national wealth.

In 1966, owing to his sympathy to the cause of the communists in Vietnam, Nkrumah left Ghana for Hanoi at the invitation of President Ho Chi Minh, to offer a solution to Vietnam. There were rumors that Nkrumah was also planning to send troops as well. On February 24 1966, Colonel Emmanuel Kotoka and Akwesi Afrifa with the help of the National police ousted Nkrumah. Afrifa and Kotoka felt that Vietnam was too complicated for Ghanaian involvement. Owing to American interest and engagement in Vietnam, the coup was given a hasty American blessing.

The young Sierra Leone army officers believed the West would embrace young radicals seeking an end to a chronic one-party system, whose failings provoked the civil war. At 10:00 p.m. on the night of April 28, 1992, Captain Musa, Second Lieutenants Nyuma and Sandy commandeered weapons and two trucks full of loyal soldiers and set out for Freetown. Troops exclusively loyal to the junior officers were briefed of the discreet mission at Joru junction on their way to Freetown.

That same night, Cobra battalion's second in command, Major S. B. Kanu, was traveling en route from the battalion headquarters in Kenema to the frontline on board a truck loaded with mortars, RPG bombs, AK-47 rifles, boxes of ammunition, anti-aircraft ammunition, grenades, rum and fuel. He bumped into the coup plotters heading for the capital city. Major Kanu attempted to intercept the officers. His orders were defied. Instead, he was wrestled and taken hostage, his truck full of supplies providing additional arsenal.

During the brief fracas to subdue Major Kanu, a handful of his bodyguards escaped to headquarters in Kenema to brief authorities of the incident. Cobra battal-

Trial by Rebellion

ion adjutant released a priority radio message to the army headquarters, informing them of young officers armed to the teeth heading for the capital city. Senior officers at headquarters had no clue why a convoy of armed soldiers led by junior officers was heading for the capital city, nor had a matching force to deny them entry into the capital.

An infantry platoon and a section of military police were instructed by the military high command to intercept the coup plotters' convoy. The interception force was effortlessly brushed aside. The coup plotters headed for and occupied the State House, seized the government-run radio station as well as other key government buildings without incident.

By mid-afternoon, the British Broadcasting Corporation (BBC) aired an incorrect version of events in Freetown, claiming a group of rebel soldiers had stormed the capital demanding better wages. The group was indeed a rebellious one, but their intentions were grossly misrepresented. The coup was a well-crafted affair aimed at overthrowing President Momoh by force if need be.

President Momoh's whereabouts were unknown at the time. A handfull of senior officers, including Lieutenant Colonel Yahya Kanu, Brigadier J.O.Y. Turay, and Major Kelly Conteh, tried to pacify the young officers to call off what they thought was a mutiny. The young officers sought defectors from among senior officers, but none came forward. Lieutenant Colonel Kanu, who was presumed to be a radical frontline commander, proved to be a disappointment, retaining his loyalty to Momoh.

Kanu made his position clear in an interview to the BBC, stating that he was not the presumed leader of the coup. His attitude mirrors most senior officers at that critical moment, reflecting the extent of fear those officers had been subjected to.

In the late afternoon frontline co-conspirators streamed into Freetown en masse. Notable citizens, college students and other anti-APC supporters took to the streets in celebration, legitimizing the official end of Momoh's APC government. President Momoh fled to neighboring Guinea. Ongoing negotiations between senior officers and the young radical officers were called off. Captains Strasser and Musa decided to take the leadership mantle. The massive outpouring of support for the regime stamped the seal of approval for political change.

Freetown does not represent Sierra Leone as a whole, but the political views of its residents mirror the mood of the nation. The euphoria of Freetown residents on April 29, 1992, aligned itself into the contours of Sierra Leone's political transformation. The bravery of the young officers exposed the weak state of Sierra Leone's army leadership. It explains why Sankoh penetrated the Sierra Leone borders with such ease.

The people of Sierra Leone openly embraced political changeover by a coup because they saw no other options for constitutional change. The constitution was irrelevant. Judicial interpretation of laws and administrative procedures were enforced to suit the whims and caprices of government. Gross abuse of executive pow-

Trial by Rebellion

ers had reduced the constitution to an ordinary legal document containing fine language, in shades of black and white theoretical constructs.

It is almost impossible to write the complete modern history of Sierra Leone without weaving the drama of April 28–29, 1992, into it. The coup dramatically altered Sierra Leone's stagnant political landscape.

Chapter 13

The overthrow of President Momoh's government was unconstitutional, however, there was a moral and ethical justification for the action. Sierra Leone was a failed state with multiple organic problems Momoh's administration could not solve. Economic stagnation was unbearable. The savagery of his economic policies manifested itself in the wide class disparity between the poor majority and rich minority. Fiscal indiscipline pulled the diamond rich Sierra Leone to the very bottom of the United Nation's cast of the world's poorest on the earth. Corruption and fiscal mismanagement was a far worse evil than the unconstitutional termination of the government that condoned it.

Public opinion, the RUF and young radical military officers shared one common belief: the need for an immediate political change. Votes and the voice of public opinion were powerless in a one-party state. Unlike Sankoh and his guerrillas who opted for the long route to power by marching to Freetown through the jungle, brutally victimizing the very people whose support he needed, the youthful military officers took the issues affecting the people directly to the APC government. The coup was swift and almost bloodless.

The coup leaders handpicked a mix of predominantly young officers and civilians, forming the National Provisional Ruling Council (NPRC). The NPRC governed by military decrees after suspending the 1978 constitution. The military council hastily convocated to draft a political agenda to meet the nation's enthusiasm for change. Topmost on the agenda was ending the war with Sankoh's RUF and eradicating corruption in government.

A high level of massive youth support and volunteerism echoed an appetizing desire for political change nationwide. The youths rendered a hand to the new regime by launching self-help initiatives aggressively cleaning the city's filth, as part of the drive to get rid of the decadence of the old government. Freetown and other major towns took on a new face. Paintings of heroes beautified the once filthy city streets. A new socio-political consciousness was born.

Diplomats in Sierra Leone frowned at the new military regime. The diplomatic community and its allied institutions have always opposed military coups in Africa. Yet they have witnessed the prostitution and plunder of Africa's resources by its corrupt leaders. Popular support for the military regime inevitably convinced Western diplomats to subscribe to the regime as the legitimate representation of the wishes of the people. The diplomatic community reluctantly traded recognition of the regime in exchange for a return to civilian democratic governance within a four-year time frame.

The reluctance to recognize massive popular support of the military coup as a means of political change questions the meaning and interpretation of political sovereignty. Mass support or consent, the likes seen on the streets of Freetown on April 29,1992, is an exclusive right of citizens of sovereign nations. Like all sovereign nations, massive solidarity of its people in support or opposition to political change should not be subjected to international questioning for approval, nor limited to the form of change its citizens see fit to support.

The reaction of the diplomatic community in Sierra Leone following the NPRC revolution was akin to neo-imperialistic propensities. It is hard to understand why the diplomatic community reserved its criticism of the Momoh administration. The strong presence of economic collapse and increasing poverty provokes a whole new question about the role and interest of the Western diplomatic community. The direct or indirect involvement of the West in determining the form of government or change amounts to hijacking the self-determination of independent nations.

One of Africa's notable civilian postcolonial leaders, President Julius Nyerere of Tanzania, once noted, "there is nothing inherently sacred about the civilian and there is nothing inherently evil about the military government. Some of the most corrupt and reactionary regimes in Africa are, or have been, headed by civilians. We must not take an oversimplified or automatic view about the merits or demerits of civilian or military government in Africa. It does not follow that the civilian government will serve the people of Africa better. Given our present stage of development, the thing that should guide our judgment in this matter is the extent to which an African government, whether civilian or military, is genuinely working in the interest of the African peoples." Military or civilian, socialist, communist, liberal, democrat or a hybrid, the best government should be evaluated on the basis of quantitative and qualitative deliverables allocated to the poor majority of African people.

Checks and balances have never been practically functional in most of postcolonial Africa. The executive branch of government in most African nations had excessive power and dominance over the legislature and the judiciary. The legislature and the judiciary were reduced to footstools at the behest of the executive. Military governments emerged in African politics as an interim measure, to check the excesses of the executive branch of government.

Momoh's government was a paradigm of an extremely powerful executive. The legislative and judiciary branch of its one-party government was an extended tentacle of the executive. No government is above conformity to law. Momoh inherited a government that was unquestionable by the judiciary. By default, such a political system was characterized by a breakdown of the system of checks and balances.

Sierra Leone's politico-military revolution was therefore an opportunity worth embracing, as a means to permanently castrate the lingering culture of overbearing executive power and corruption in the public sector. It was a perfect time to deconstruct aged public policy in preparation for a new model. The threat to Sierra

Leone's political renewal was the resolve of the old society, and the determination of its attendant institutions to put up a socio-organic resistance.

Cleaning up corruption and uprooting the vestiges of the old society warranted a tough hand and absolute support to uphold the changes. A new model was required to undo the stagnation in the public sector.

The termination of Momoh's administration was simply an end to one of Sierra Leone's many challenges. Mapping a new political roadmap presented another. The transition period turned out to unearth the bitterest conflicts between the forces of the old and new youthful military government.

The young military leadership was threatened by the aged African tradition that dismisses the eligibility, wisdom and value of youthful leadership. In the context of the typical African political systems, young men and women had no place in national leadership roles. As with most old societies, the forces of the old Sierra Leone were poised to challenge the young dynamic leadership change, regardless of the immediate and long-term benefits.

There was no constructive gubernatorial agenda at the inception of the provisional government. The younger military government officials relied on the wisdom of the notable civilians appointed to the governing council. In his first speech, Chairman Strasser promised a speedy conclusion of the war, offering an olive branch to the RUF. The immediate reaction of the RUF to the overthrow of the APC was promising. Sankoh announced an unofficial ceasefire, referring to the NPRC as his "brothers in arms."

The nexus of peace in Sierra Leone was wholly dependent on the pacification of Foday Sankoh, but whether it was a case of bad counsel, political immaturity, or lack of strategic foresight, the NPRC misplaced peace as a military and political priority. The NPRC failed to seriously engage and exploit Sankoh's ceasefire overtures as a path to peace. The NPRC government aligned itself with its neighboring Anglophone militocracy, pursuing a military option to the conflict.

As much as the NPRC nursed the will to fulfill its revolutionary promises, the genuine intents of the new administration met tumultuous obstacles from its collocation with the old order. Carved from long years of APC partisanship, the neutrality of the civil service had been compromised by years of patronage. Co-option of the aged civil service system with the NPRC administration was the equivalent of prescribing a cough syrup for knee pain.

Undoing the corrupted civil service infrastructure was key to Sierra Leone's socio-political renewal. It required an immediate staff cleansing, structural reengineering and process redesign. The revival of neutrality in the civil service was grounded in a complete overhaul of the system, recruiting a new crop of civil servants to operate on a new model. Like its predecessor, the NPRC retained the existing civil service and tried micromanaging it. The problem remained incurable.

Chapter 14

A quick fix to the Sankoh-led rebellion was hidden in the wisdom of negotiations tempered with limited conditions. The ugly presence of a political resistance, its destabilizing effect in regions vital to the nation's economy was worthy of negotiation.

Of course the RUF had evolved into a force immune to elimination on the battlefield overnight. In the interest of the safety of poor farmers and the strain on the national economy, it was reasonably justified to engage and negotiate with the RUF. The ultimate objective should have revolved around a gradual cessation of hostilities, discussion of the frustrations and the very causes of the uprising, reconciliation and eventual power sharing by an interim administration. The interim administration should have laid the foundation for a new political start, free of one dominant political party system.

Revved by the promise of full military support from Nigeria's President General Ibrahim B. Babangida and Ghana's Flight Lieutenant Jerry J. Rawlings, the NPRC pursued a full-scale military confrontation with Sankoh's RUF. The NPRC procured a huge cache of arms and ammunition, including Russian tanks and helicopters, for major offensives into the RUF heartland.

The military regime also increased wages in the public sector including the army by one hundred percent, further bolstering support for the regime.

The NPRC's indefinite suspension of communications with the RUF and its pursuit of a military option, amounted to its fundamental political error. The radical view of the young military government had been favorable to make amends with the RUF, but the idea suddenly took a different turn. The overshadowing influence of Anglophone allies whose unofficial policy was opposed to compromise with Taylor and Sankoh took precedence. A joint offensive with Nigerian overhead air and artillery support was plotted into "Operation Destroy All," scaled for the rebel stronghold of Pendembu in the Kailahun district.

RUF intelligence was starved of information on the mode and timing of the joint operation. The RUF was not anticipating nor prepared for a large-scale assault from the new administration. The secrecy, level of detailed planning, new weaponry, high morale and speed of the army's advance left the RUF with no defensive strategy and manpower to counter the surprise attack. The recapture of Pendembu was swift.

Troop occupation of Pendembu presented a unique opportunity that could have forced the RUF organizational foundation out of commission. RUF's access to Charles Taylor in Liberia was strategically vital to its continued survival. Targeting the access routes with unremitting aggression should have starved the RUF of direct NPFL support. The pursuit of a full-scale assault

Trial by Rebellion

on all of RUF's Kailahun strongholds, including its re-supply route from across Liberia, was never fully explored.

While it was militarily prudent to consolidate its hold on Pendembu, the army should have upheld the momentum and pursued disoriented RUF fighters in their state of instability. A complete demolition of the RUF headquarters would have psychologically ruined the movement's foundation.

RUF's territorial stake was threatened by the capture of Pendembu. It sent a militarily sound but politically incorrect message to the RUF. It meant negotiations and the possibility of a dialogue was no longer an option. Pendembu emboldened Strasser to drop the olive branch, urging the RUF to surrender. The solicitation to surrender angered the RUF. More than anything else, it meant a complete exclusion from the political process and further criminalizing the rebellion.

The RUF had expected that the NPRC would embrace the rationale of a peaceful conclusion of the war by sharing power, as opposed to the continued use of force. The attack dealt a blow into the central cord of the RUF's political expectations, dismissing hopes of further talks.

Following the recapture of the rebel stronghold of Pendembu, the new head of state paid a visit to troops on the forward edge of the front. The visit honors Strasser as the bravest Sierra Leonean president yet, the first to ever tread a battlefield, in sharp contrast to his predecessor. It reenergized the troops.

The army's brief operational pause following the recapture of Pendembu, gave the RUF time to regroup. Sankoh was forced to consult with Taylor regarding the RUF's next course of action. NPRC's pro-military action cornered the RUF into a position of desperation. The RUF's reaction to hostilities by the military government was the publication of "Footpath to Democracy." It was the RUF's first official document publicizing its frustrations than its ideology.

"Footpath to Democracy" labeled the NPRC a continuum of the APC government, accusing it as, "a cast in the image of his master." Sankoh castigated the NPRC as "military adventurists" and "watch dogs of the APC." The RUF leadership alleged that the NPRC was a protectionist force, guarding a long standing contractual agreement between the army and the APC. The sense of frustration was made manifest by strong anti-NPRC sentiments, registered in the second verse of RUF's revolutionary song.

Trial by Rebellion

RUF/SL Anthem

RUF is fighting to save Sierra Leone
RUF is fighting to save our people
RUF is fighting to save our country
RUF is fighting to save Sierra Leone
Chorus:
Go and tell the President, Sierra Leone is my home
Go and tell my parents, they may see me no more
When fighting in the battlefield I'm fighting forever
Every Sierra Leonean is fighting for his land

Where are our diamonds, Mr. President?
Where is our gold, NPRC?
RUF is hungry to know where they are
RUF is fighting to save Sierra Leone
Our people are suffering without means of survival
All our minerals have gone to foreign lands
RUF is hungry to know where they are
RUF is fighting to save Sierra Leone
Sierra Leone is ready to utilise her own
All our minerals will be accounted for
The people will enjoy in their land
RUF is the saviour we need right now
RUF is fighting to save Sierra Leone
RUF is fighting to save our people
RUF is fighting to save our country

Chapter 15

In April 1993, the NPRC celebrated a year in office with demonstrable accomplishments. As a part of its celebrations, the NPRC government announced the release of all former APC government ministers held on corruption charges. In a year, the economy bounced from the inherited decline of the APC government's mismanagement. With parts of the country destabilized by rebel activities, inflation was drastically reduced from 119 percent in 1991 to 25 percent in 1993, outpacing the International Monetary Fund's (IMF) forecasted expectations.

Trade was liberalized, removing restrictions on the flow of foreign currency. Foreign exchange rates stabilized, and the price of a bag of rice, the staple food, dropped from fifteen thousand Leones (Le 15,000) per kg bag to a stable rate of eight thousand Leones (Le 8,000). Back-dated wages of government employees were paid up to date. Dead or fictitious employees on government payroll suddenly disappeared into oblivion and subsequent wages were paid on time. Electricity supply increased, water supply improved, and transportation cost remained unchanged even with the increase in the price of gasoline. After years of inactivity, the nation's only television station came back on the air.

It was impossible to turn the economy around in 365 days after taking over from the fiscally irresponsible APC government, while spending well over half a million dollars a month on defense. Consumer price index (CPI) was not significantly impacted by changes in fiscal policy, but indiscriminate price fluctuation of consumer goods was contained.

Imports continued to outpace exports because of the logistical needs of the ongoing war and the loss of agricultural productivity and significant mining areas. The deficit was rolled back by three percent in a year compared to the outgoing APC government's 67 percent.

By his own admission, RUF leader Foday Sankoh noted that "by late 1993 we (RUF) had been forced to beat a hasty retreat as successful infiltration almost destroyed our ranks. We were pushed to the border with Liberia. Frankly, we were beaten and were on the run but our pride and deep sense of calling would not let us face the disgrace of crossing into Liberia as refugees or prisoners of war." This was indication the army under the NPRC government almost annihilated the RUF. The movement was on the verge of crumbling.

The next two years following its first anniversary were full of new challenges. The advent of the military government came with regimental indiscipline and problems with public relations. Military personnel attached to government officers became unruly, untouchable and disrespectful of regimental seniority. Then Major Kelly Conteh spoke out to the threats military politics posed to regimental discipline. The head of state ordered the execution of three unruly soldiers by firing squad, as an example of his resolve to deal with the issue of indiscipline.

The NPRC government also appointed Major Kelly Conteh as the army's chief of staff to restore the culture of regimental discipline. Conteh's transformation from the cream of the APC army to the very crust of the NPRC government exemplified the NPRC's desire to amalgamate the experience of the old school to restore regimental order. Conteh failed to address the issue of indiscipline because he had no direct control over the security personnel of NPRC government officials, who were the perpetrators of regimental deviance.

He resorted to a strategy of separating the army from the military government instead of addressing the source of the problem. Politics and split loyalty divided the army into two camps. It cannibalized the synergy of the army at large and gradually impacted total support for the NPRC.

The political climate evolved into a fanfare of different forces at loggerheads with each other. The NPRC versus itself on one hand; against the RUF, the main stream army, dethroned APC politicians and the press on the other hand. The Chairman of the NPRC, Captain Valentine Strasser was reluctant to pursue alternative approaches to ending the conflict with Sankoh, including consent with members of his government over a possible dialogue with the rebels.

Differences between the Head of State, Captain Valentine Strasser and his deputy, Captain Solomon A. J.

Musa, distracted the focus on the war. Conflict between the two was mostly borne out of disagreement over policy directives and individual expectations. Captain Musa felt his boss was a dormant, ineffective military leader. Strasser felt his deputy exhibited hard-line political extremism near over ambition.

The conflict between Strasser and Musa gradually ballooned into an intense armed standoff that may have resulted in a bloody political catastrophe. The Head of State swung into action quickly relieving his deputy of his duties. The difficulty was disarming bodyguards to the Deputy of Head of State. His heavily armed guards were prepared to face off with those of the head of state. Between the two leaders, the arsenal of arms and ammunition in their custody was the most sophisticated in the nation. Captain Musa voluntarily called off the standoff and left for London. The shakeup peeled away the cohesiveness of the NPRC government.

Against the backdrop of a military government and its army divided by politics, discord and indiscipline, Sankoh outlined the RUF's resurging strategy in *Footpath to Democracy*. "We (RUF) dispersed into smaller units, whatever remained of our fighting force. The civilians were advised to abandon the towns and cities, which they did. We destroyed all our vehicles and heavy weapons that would retard our progress as well as expose our locations. We now relied on light weapons and on our feet, brains and knowledge of the countryside. We moved deeper into the comforting bosom of our mother earth - the forest".

Trial by Rebellion

A special RUF task force infiltrated all military deployments to attack the resourceful and politically sensitive mining and commercial townships. RUF forces advanced northwest of Kailahun, bypassing military deployments to hit the overpopulated, diamond-rich Kono district. The RUF assault on the rich diamond-mining district impacted national revenue and commerce.

The RUF tapped into the resources of the overpopulated Kono district, beefing up its manpower by recruiting fighters to resist the army's attempts to recapture the mines and conscripted laborers to aggressively mine diamonds. The mining landscape laced with huge piles of dirt and cavernous holes, served as cover from fire. With the civilian population out of the town, the RUF pitched camp, making the Kono Township the most complex theater of combat.

Knowing the value of Kono to the nation's economic survival, the RUF guerrillas were undeniably convinced the army would allocate every resource at its disposal to recapture the mines. To create a buffer for RUF fighters overseeing its labor force in the mines, a strong contingent of RUF rebels advanced towards the capital city, capturing hold of Okra Hill, to force a diversion of government troops away from Kono.

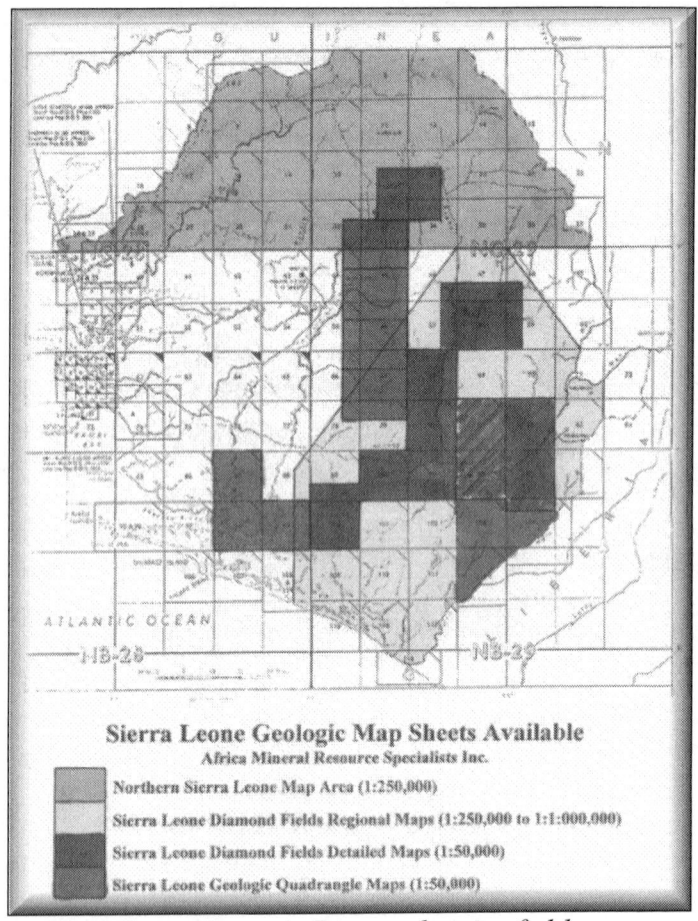

Sierra Leone's Diamond major fields

The RUF occupation of Okra hill was a tactical obstacle created to demoralize troop reinforcements bound for Kono, by incessant attacks and lethal ambushes along the strategic highway to Kono. The RUF's presence thirty-eight miles outside the capital Freetown and its unrelenting hold on the Kono diamond mines paralyzed the NPRC's ability to contain the situation. The bulk of its troops were consumed in defense of captured ground further east and south.

Concerned about the precarious position of the government's primary source of revenue, the army recruited the services of traditional hunters to help destabilize the RUF in Kono. While the army focused its resources on regaining the diamond mines of Kono, RUF rebels spread further inland toward Makeni, Kabala, Port Loko and Kambia in the north, Mile 91, Mysiaka, Sierra Rutile, Moyamba and Songo in the west toward the capital.

The farther into the interior RUF advanced, the more they sensed the weaknesses of the army. Rather than relying on support from its Kailahun headquarters for re-supply, RUF rebels resorted to ambushing both civilian transports and military convoys along key commercial highways.

The army reacted by providing heavily armed escorts to protect commercial vehicles to the provinces. The approach was costly, highly risky and counterproductive. Army escorts were ambushed. Commercial drivers and passengers were mostly the victims of the ambushes. The RUF intercepted and burnt vehicles, used the carcasses to block the highway, grabbed food, money and abducted harmless civilians especially women, killing those who resisted capture. The guerrillas also donned military uniforms to attack civilians in townships, fomenting civilian animosity for the army.

NPRC's popularity slowly faded away as the RUF drilled fear into the civil population. The pulse of the media gave Sankoh another strategic tool. He exploited the media to disseminate misinformation designed to embitter civil military relations. Diligent army officers were framed as rebel collaborators.

Lieutenant Colonel Chernor Dean was one such victim. Ambushed by RUF rebels on the Makeni highway, his abandonment of a vehicle full of ammunition was interpreted as collaboration with the RUF. He was court-martialed and sentenced to death without a shred of evidence linking him to the RUF organization. Lieutenant Daniel Tallover was also victimized by similar allegations. He was arrested and quarantined as a suspected rebel collaborator.

The RUF had orchestrated a similar scheme in Panguma under the command of Lieutenant Philip Forbie, following the death of Father McAllister. Against RUF's advertised reputation for savage brutality, the innocence of army officers was tampered by the growing bias of public opinion.

The RUF also targeted Lieutenant Colonel Tom Nyuma, a highly respected member of the NPRC government. Appointed undersecretary of defense to deal with RUF's renewed threats, he believed in his experience, his men and guts to lead forces in battle, regardless of his political appointment. With almost every confrontation against the RUF in his favor, he became a victim of unfounded allegations that he was in cahoots with RUF rebels.

Trial by Rebellion

Without sifting through the strings of allegations with a sense of caution, a smear campaign was launched to victimize Sierra Leone's finest army officers. Some independent newspapers unfairly publicized irrational opinions far from the truth. The army found no voice to defend its own at the destructive hands of RUF's propaganda.

By implicating national characters and destabilizing key areas of national commercial interest, especially the diamond mines of Tongo and Kono, the bauxite and rutile deposits in Moyamba, including major roads networks, Sankoh took the nation's economy hostage. Trust in the army's ability to contain the war was completely lost to the pandemonium of RUF activities.

Chapter 16

The gradual exodus of RUF's guerillas first from across the Liberian border, then through the maze of troops in deployment into every corner of the north, south and central Sierra Leone was well managed. Unlike the army, RUF guerillas used the jungle effectively. It was extremely difficult for the army to cover enough ground to deter RUF infiltrations. Part of the complexity to contain RUF infiltration was their resolve to mobilize on foot through the jungle in small teams, with arms and ammunition that weighed an average of thirty pounds per man. In plain civilian clothes, they could deceptively pass as locals.

In the absence of a swift means of mobility from its Kailahun headquarters, the pace of RUF advances through the jungle was bound to be slow. The army was passive in its challenge to pursue the rebels in the jungle. Infantry mobilization was mostly vehicular. Troop patrols in the jungle were for the most part short lived, giving rebels a free rein to leverage the weakness.

The army's predominant tactics to the RUF's hit and run raids were reactionary rather than proactive. Defense of captured ground was typical of the army's reactionary tactics. It consumed the army's manpower and tied troops down, leaving the jungle to Sankoh's rebels. The effect; the RUF struck most major towns and villages nationwide, with the exception of the capital city, Freetown and Bo, the second largest city.

The army's intelligence unit remained dysfunctional, falling short of fulfilling its obligations to capture data on the strength, movements and habits of the RUF. The Kono mines remained a bottleneck, its occupation alternating between the army and the RUF.

RUF's persistence to retain its occupation of the mines starved government and private businesses of more than seventy percent of revenue generated from mining. The recapture, security and stability of the Kono diamond mines became a prime cause for concern. The NPRC government sought a new approach to regain the mines from RUF occupation.

Mercenary services were outsourced through a British-based supplier of military hardware. The NPRC government resolved to hire retired Ghurka elements, a Nepalese unit of the British Army, specialized in nonconventional combat techniques. Outsourcing foreign mercenaries left Sierra Leonean soldiers feeling underestimated, unappreciated and demoralized.

RUF's intelligence network got wind of mercenary activities. The government's contract of mercenaries to its aid was an indicator that the army had lost the initiative to tackle the second phase of RUF's operation. The Ghurkas conducted ad hoc training with the intent to assault RUF's impregnable Okra Hill base located thirty-nine miles outside Freetown. Okra hill was three

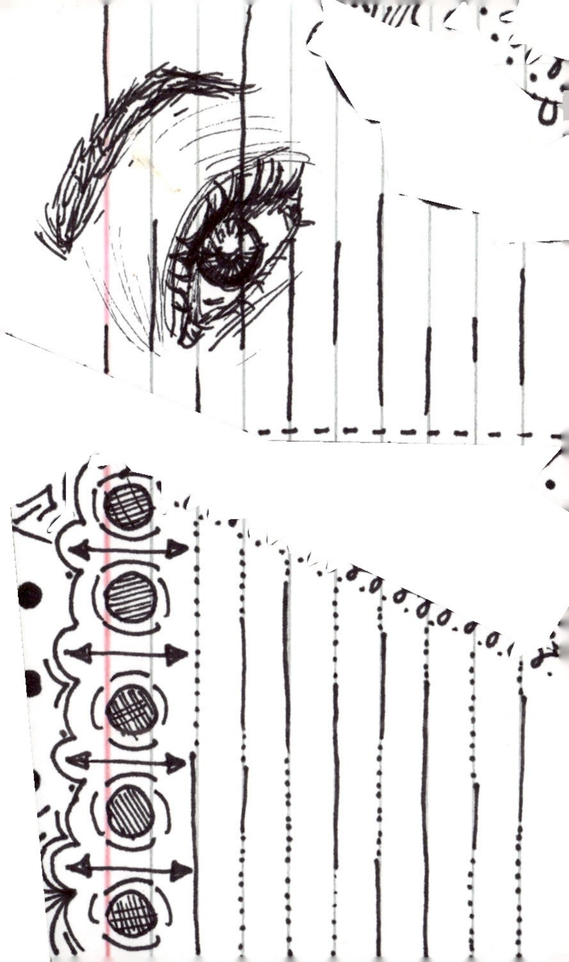

hundred feet above sea level, overlooking the entire network of commercial traffic to the north and southeast from the capital Freetown.

American born Bob McKenzie, a retired Vietnam veteran led the Ghurkas on the risk-prone mission to attack the RUF against the odds of conventional and counter-guerilla warfare. The resolve to dislodge the RUF from the Okra Hill base was simmered with strings of tactical miscalculations; primarily, the reliance on a weak and untenable intelligence.

With sketchy intelligence on the RUF's strength and no precise knowledge of the Okra Hill layout, the mission was ill conceived. The impregnable base was inaccessible to civilians and impossible for reconnaissance. It is tactically irrational to attack an enemy occupying the top of a hill. Three factors militate against such an attack. The occupying rebels commanded an excellent view, had better cover from fire and capable of moving quicker than the attacking force.

The joint army and Gurka team, barely a company strong, met a brave determined and disciplined rebel defense. The RUF initiated the firefight quickly destabilizing the joint Army-Ghurka team. McKenzie and aide to the Head of State Captain A. B. Tarawally were killed in the firefight, robbing the joint team of command and control. The withdrawal of remaining element was disorganized with rebels in pursuit.

On the orders of the RUF leader Foday Sankoh, McKenzie's remains were transported to the RUF camp in Kailahun, to be used as a propaganda feat. The high-profile casualties struck the military administration very hard. The fumbled operation was suppressed by the military regime, but the painful loss of the president's aide could not be concealed. The Ghurka operation was quietly laid to rest after the funeral of the president's aide.

There were several tactical options to evicting the RUF from its Okra Hill base prone to less risk. The base should have been surrounded and suppressed with artillery fire before an assault. A larger force should have approached the base from several flanks and engaged the rebels from a distance to force the RUF to deplete their ammunition holdings, before attempting an assault.

News of the high valued casualties boosted the fighting spirit of the RUF, giving them a new resolve to make further advances towards Freetown. By December 1994, the enthusiasm of the military regime was overshadowed by RUF's propaganda, unpopular public opinion and the lost love of the press for the military regime.

Once again the RUF regained a healthy dose of momentum. The NPRC government was momentarily frozen by the new dilemma. Its popularity dwindled by its incapacity to arrest and contain the RUF's renewed onslaughts. To address the situation, the NPRC contracted the services of the South Africa-based Executive Outcomes; a private mercenary firm to rescue the situation.

Tony Buckingham, a veteran of the British SAS put together a small group of South African soldiers of fortune, to train Sierra Leone soldiers and liberate the Kono mines from RUF occupation.

Trial by Rebellion

Strasser agreed to finance the Executive Outcomes operations on credit, with a promise of US$500,000 a month to be paid in the form of diamond concessions to Branch Energy, a subsidiary of DeBeers. The World Bank and the International Monetary Fund (IMF) were privy to the agreement. Armed with helicopter gun ships and a wealth of jungle warfare experience from Angola, the RUF was forced out of the mines within three months.

Evicted from Kono by the joint army and Executive Outcomes coalition, the RUF reconfigured a new strategic focus. Sankoh engineered a new wave of rumors, threatening to capture Freetown. The city was on edge. The mountainous peninsula suburbs of Freetown witnessed the emergence of suspicious strangers. Fortunately, strangers were easily identified and arrested because the villages around the peninsula were mostly depopulated, close-knit communities whose residents knew each other.

The peninsular landscape surrounding the capital also posed a natural threat to RUF's activities. The mountains were steep, movement was slow and re-supply almost impossible. Local commerce was based largely on low-volume fishing, farming and a suffocating tourist industry. News of RUF activities around the peninsula left residents in Freetown hanging on fear and growing uncertainty, a result of the RUF's exploitation of fear as a tool of propaganda.

Penetrating the army's line of defense by infiltration as opposed to confrontation, represents the second phase of RUF operations. It was either part of a long-term strategic plan unleashed a little too early, a real desperate move to force a dialogue, or a combination of both. The RUF revved its propaganda campaign, exclusively focused on deflating the popularity of the NPRC government and threatening residents of Freetown into capitulation.

Chapter 17

The second phase of RUF operations accentuated the relative importance, capabilities and effect of psychological warfare. RUF's psychological warfare techniques remained undetected by the army. The RUF exploited the army's weak counterpropaganda to the fullest. Sankoh had recognized the unpopularity of his rebellious political cause. He resorted to mind mapping, using terror as a major component to enrage public perception of the NPRC government's powerlessness to contain his chaos. Sankoh anticipated that his brutality against lives and property would influence international and local public opinion, to pressure the NPRC government to consider a dialogue.

The longer it took Sankoh to earn political recognition, the further his fighters were driven to the edge of desperation. RUF propaganda schemes were hardly scrutinized or countered by the army. RUF guerrillas used military fatigues to attack sensitive communities with impunity, angering the public and inflaming allegations that government troops were playing dual roles as RUF rebels.

An effective counterstrategy to RUF's use of military fatigues could have been an unannounced switch to another shade of camouflage in the entire frontline, to allay the suspicions of the public. That may have helped distinguish rebels using military fatigues. The army was particularly reckless in its management and audit of its entire communications network, supplies, especially fatigues and ammunition.

RUF's continued chaos, misinformation and growing public suspicions, amplified by unsubstantiated belief that soldiers were acting dual roles as RUF rebels, subjected Foday Sankoh's existence to further doubts. Public opinion perceived the elusive Sankoh as a fictitious character invented by the army to induce fear into the population. The percentage of the population convinced of Sankoh's existence was miniscule.

Sankoh successfully waged an intellectual war of grand psychological proportions, engaging the army in firefights not for conquest, but to retain the perception that his forces were unbeatable in combat. Knowing the army's conventional mode of operation, Sankoh capitalized on his previous experiences to tap into the army's ever increasing weaknesses.

He succeeded in manipulating Sierra Leoneans to see the NPRC as the political problem and not the ascribed liberators. The indiscriminate sequence of RUF attacks in communities far away from their Kailahun headquarters gave credence to the psychological farce. The brewing soldier/rebel allegations gave rise to the "sobel" acronym, setting the scene for Sankoh's psychological victory. Pro-APC loyalists echoed anti-NPRC sentiments in areas where the RUF could not operate. Sankoh successfully won his bid to manipulate public opinion to defame the army in a society where logical reasoning had little or no foundation.

The press reported facts, rumors and innuendoes unintentionally favorable to RUF's strategic aims. Anti-NPRC sentiments in the press deflated the NPRC's enthusiasm and accomplishments. The reaction of public opinion offered Sankoh the feedback he needed to reinforce terror as a tool of choice.

NPRC Chairman Strasser remained hesitant to talk to Sankoh for fear of falling out of favor with his Anglophone counterparts. It was a risky venture not knowing Sankoh's motives, but the rewards to negotiate far outweighed the risks. It was worth a try. Though not guaranteed, cessation of hostilities and a continuous engagement with the rebels could have saved lots of lives and properties.

Strasser opted to offer Sankoh and his fighters amnesty and room to transform his movement into a political party in preparation for upcoming elections. Sankoh was uncomfortable with Strasser's narrow overtures. Sankoh preferred political recognition through direct talks and subsequent power sharing. Sankoh needed ample time to mend fences and inject his rationale for the war to the larger public.

The pressure of RUF offensives, public distrust and internal fracas among members within the military administration undermined the NPRC's organizational synergy. Defense undersecretary Captain Kumba Kambo resigned out of frustration. These strings of interrelated events clouded the political climate with loads of uncertainties and loss of faith in the competence of the military government to end the war.

Like all military dictatorships, Strasser governed by decree, not consent, distancing himself from his colleagues. The Supreme Council of State, the executive body of the military regime, was crippled to inertia. Strasser became a bourgeoisie, distancing himself from the people, one of the greatest flaws of his and any revolution.

Strasser intended to shed his military uniform and transform the NPRC to a political party with a predominant civilian composition. The intended transformation was practically awkward, given the NPRC's growing unpopularity. The move presented politicians an opportunity to further politicize and castigate the NPRC government's failures.

Unlike contemporary military governments in Africa, the NPRC was sensitive to its image in the press and overly tolerant to criticism. The newspaper, *For Di People*, championed the media war, provoking public sentiment through political cartoons, ballooning complaints involving uniformed men. Rightly so, most of the vigilantes allowed to use military fatigues and carry weapons used it indiscriminately for extra judicial purposes. Civilians were threatened and old personal scores settled. In the eyes of the media and its audience, the military government was to blame.

The patriotic sacrifice of soldiers in the frontline was painfully overlooked in the emerging political hurricane.

It was very difficult to change the contorted vision of a sensitive and suspicious public.

Strasser's publicized political intentions gave birth to a third rebellion; an elitist–movement comprising a loose union of prospective politicians from various parties whose creed was targeted at ending military rule. For the first time in Sierra Leone, civil political activists challenged Africa's trend of metamorphosing military governments into civilian regimes.

Chapter 18

By early 1996, RUF rebels had built a solid rumor platform for a psychological invasion of the capital city. RUF rebel activities around the immediate suburbs posed a major psychological threat to the relative stability of Freetown. The RUF targeted attacks on villages close to Lungi international airport and Benguma military training camp, both located a few kilometers outside Freetown.

The attack on the military school was specifically designed to collect intelligence on military training activities and explore the possibility of securing ammunition. The raids crumbled on low ammunition and a stout defense put up by the army.

Sankoh had estimated that a premature assault on Freetown would likely fail, not because of logistical constraints alone. Small rebel teams holding low ammunition stock on foot patrol were limited by slow mobility and deficient communications.

Additionally, his movement had no sympathizers in and around Freetown. RUF rebels were not familiar with, nor had a strategy to tackle the geography and demographic complexity of Freetown.

The capital city was locked behind a cocoon of rocky plateaus, unfriendly vegetations and a sprawling marshy swampland flanked by the open jaws of the Atlantic Ocean. Two major highways leading to the capital were fortified by joint Nigerian and Sierra Leonean army checkpoints. RUF's quest to penetrate Freetown was strangled by these natural and man-made obstacles.

At the height of Sankoh's drive to penetrate the capital city, the NPRC government was tethered in a heated dissension over handing power to a democratically elected civilian leadership. At stake; whether it was the right time for transition to a civilian democratic government given RUF's threat to the capital city.

Strasser's political advisers forged ahead with the metamorphosis of the military regime to a civilian administration. Strasser had already resorted to discard the consent of his key military government officers on the issue of his political future. The developments fermented uneasy tensions, which resulted in a split of the military regime into two camps.

The Head of State's camp sought political continuity from a military to civilian administration. The deputy Head of State's camp was keen on talks with Sankoh to ensure a cessation of hostilities as a precursor to the elections, before the transfer of power to a civilian regime and subsequent return to barracks.

Strasser initiated his transition program by dishing out compensatory military ranks to fellow revolutionaries, with triple promotions from captains to Lieutenant

Colonels. The officers were to relinquish political offices to assume military appointments in Sierra Leone's first Defense Headquarters. The Deputy Head of State J. M. Bio was appointed Chief of Defense Staff, with military members of the NPRC serving as defense staff officers. The army, navy, and a skeletal helicopter crew labeled the air wing, became separate administrative entities, answerable to the Chief of Defense Staff.

The reorganization and reallocation of power was not well received by most of the older staff officers. The traditional power of the Chief of Army Staff was now subjected to another layer of military authority, creating a barrier between the Army Chief of Staff's traditional access to political authorities.

As the dust settled on the dynamic institutional reorganization, a highly classified information regarding the intents of the Head of State fell through the cracks. Staff officers of the newly designed defense headquarters, all of whom were still active members of the NPRC government, were reliably informed that Strasser had planned on dismissing all the NPRC military officers from the defense headquarters. The motive was unclear, but it may have been a way to deflate the threats his colleagues would pose to his prospective civilian presidency.

In reaction to the information, the Deputy Head of State and Chief of Defense Staff Brigadier J. M. Bio rallied his key staff officers, disarmed Strasser's personal security in less than 60 minutes, handcuffed the Head of State and escorted him out of his cocoon of political power at gunpoint to neighboring Guinea.

In his subsequent radio address, Bio informed the nation that his resolve to overthrow the head of state was precipitated by his desire to see the return of the country to civilian-elected administration. That statement was open to many interpretation and speculations. The political pulse in the nation at the time of Strasser's overthrow was characterized by suspicions about Bio's motives at the eleventh hour of the NPRC's lifespan. The public held the conviction that the deposed Strasser was a victim of power-hungry and deceitful comrades.

The palace coup and immediacy to initiate talks with Sankoh were equally viewed as a strategic ploy to extend the life of the NPRC's hold on power. Regardless of the perception of public opinion, Bio pursued a dialogue with Sankoh through the mediatory assistance of the government of the Ivory Coast.

In 1996, the NPRC officially gave Sankoh audience. Sankoh's recognition ushered in a temporary calm in all fronts. As much as Bio was eager to engage the RUF leadership, Sankoh was equally eager to talk. With strategic custody of resourceful sectors of the country contributing to national revenue, Sankoh realized the sacred value of chaos and violence as a vital bargaining chip. To publicize the transparency of the occasion, owing to reigning suspicions that the NPRC government had been hyping the war to retain power, members of the press were invited to witness the talks with Sankoh over military radio. Newspapers headlines the following morning finally put an end to the public's disbelief that the rebel leader was dead or a fictitious character created by the army.

Trial by Rebellion

Ongoing talks with Sankoh did not freeze preparations for pending elections. The international community was watching and waiting to see the reation of the military government. Sankoh expressed his bitter dissatisfaction at Bio's urgency to push for elections, without peacefully ironing out the conflict. Sankoh repeatedly emphasized the irrationality of rushing to turn over power to politicians, claiming that power would end up in the hands of the same old order.

Sankoh had a strong preference for peace to precede the elections, but an unofficial referendum of community, religious and political leaders voted in favor of "Elections before Peace." Politics snuffed out the meaningful value of peace at the time. Popular support for "Elections before Peace" was a collective activist reaction to the suspicions levied against Bio's military-led government and the inadequacies of his case for ousting Strasser. Public outcry for "Elections before Peace" was also a campaign to undo the intended notion of transforming the uniformed military government into a subsequent civilian-elected government.

Commencement of the voter registration process following the "Elections before Peace" referendum enraged Sankoh all over again. In response, the RUF unleashed a new form of terror campaign, sadistically cutting off arms, legs, and fingers to frighten the electorate to reverse their preference for "Elections before Peace." Sankoh instituted the new carnage to give Bio a perfect excuse to either hold off the ongoing electoral process, postpone or even cancel the elections.

The diplomatic community microscopically watched the unfolding political drama. The RUF's renewed psychology of inhumane violence in no way crippled public enthusiasm and determination to forge ahead with elections, nor did it influence Bio to postpone or suspend the elections.

In fairness to all the political parties, including the RUF, there was not enough time to plan for the elections, raise funds, campaign and give every Sierra Leonean their constitutional right to vote. Insecurity limited the movement of political parties to campaign nationwide. Sierra Leoneans behind rebel lines and most refugees were unable to register nor in a position to vote.

The elections were held as scheduled but not without problems. Pro-military government supporters incited unruly soldiers to disrupt the elections. Come election day, Bio's official home was attacked by a handful of unknown soldiers. Election results returned the SLPP candidate Ahmed Tejan Kabbah as the winner in a highly contested run off with the United National Peoples Party (UNPP) led by the veteran politician Dr. John Karefa Smart.

The second military leader on record after Nigeria's Olusegun Obasanjo to return power to a civilian administration, Bio gracefully handed over the baton of power under the watchful eyes of a skeptical nation. Sankoh's quest to delay the electoral process was overridden by the wishes of the people. Sankoh settled to work with the democratically elected government.

Trial by Rebellion

The RUF's survival through the leadership of Presidents Momoh, Strasser, Bio and Kabbah is not proof that the RUF had a better fighting organization or was immune to conquest. Rather, it ascertains that guerrilla warfare was by far the most intriguing mode of combat, complex to manage and almost impossible to contain.

In retrospect, an earlier engagement in talks with the RUF could have minimized the havoc on the stability and security of Sierra Leone. It did not matter what government had to forgo to save lives and property worth millions, than stand on principles to fight Sankoh to the end. The adherence to a military solution of the conflict accounted for the protraction of the violence.

Like the ousted President Momoh, the NPRC had a share of the blame for prolonging the war. The difference was the NPRC's genuineness and commitment to produce quick results. In its totality, the RUF campaign exposed the inherent deficiency of the Sierra Leone war machinery, the paucity of leaders in the army and the need for a strategic makeover of the institution.

"The most successful General," Sun-Tzu once said, "was the one who achieved his ends without battle, or with minimal losses." Bio sets himself apart from Momoh and Strasser as the general who recognized the rational and economic value of peace through negotiations. His overtures for peace did not make him soft or a coward, but an astute disciple of the Chinese military philosopher.

Foday Sankoh on his part will never be complimented for the chain of political changes his movement triggered. His transformation of Sierra Leone into killing fields, far outweighed the chronic flaws of the APC government he attempted to overthrow. The visible scars and images of severed arms and limbs of the young and old, remain a living reminder of his handiwork as well as the tactical and political miscalculations of the governments he fought.

The military is an "instrument of public policy." As much as Sierra Leone's army was led by a string of inefficient commanders, their actions like the peacekeeping forces in Liberia, were subject to the dominant political wishes of their masters. The chaos and subsequent intervention that swept the West African sub-region indeed magnifies the reality. Political decisions and the military actions of Sierra Leone's army, as well as peacekeeping forces in Liberia, mirror the sub-regional polarization and tactical miscalculation of its political leaders.

The tug of ideas between an aggressive Anglophone interventionism, versus a passive Francophone- sponsored dialogue and direct support of Taylor, highlights the extent of double standards and skewed indifferences that pervade the sub-region. Liberia's crisis exposed the sub-regional divide, the dislocation of ECOWAS, its peacekeeping forces and a single voice of consent over critical issues.

Civil wars and violent uprisings had become Africa's radical instrument of last resort to the absence of civil political change. The appeal to violent political change strongly suggests that most African governments continue to fall short of their constitutional, economic, and moral responsibilities. African leaders continue to oversee nations lagging behind the rest of the world in the provision of sustainable solutions to poverty, disease, corruption, economic inequality, social injustice, and tribalism.

This political case study serves as a living testament to the snail-paced responses and failures of sub-regional political institutions, including the United Nations. It challenges future leaders, politicians, students, anti-government forces and the international community to advocate caution or mediate civil conflicts as early as possible.

Liberian rebel Leader Charles Taylor

Sierra Leone Rebel Leader Foday Sankoh

The financier of the conflict

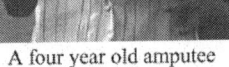

A father and his baby girl

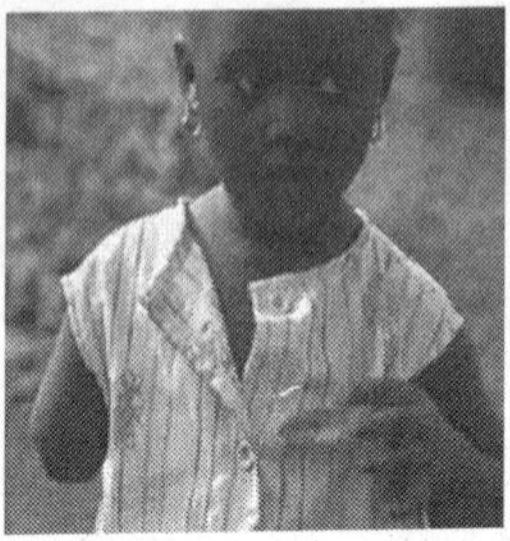

A four year old amputee

A young trader

Amputated Victims of War

Governments need not resort to armed blows with oppositions without understanding the reasoning behind the motivation to take up arms, through open honest and healthy dialogue, nor should anti-government revolutionaries take up arms to fight governments without exhausting alternative civil options.

Protracted armed conflicts victimize the innocent civilians governments claim to be protecting—the same innocent civilians liberation fighters profess to be emancipating from economic, political and social oppression.

Trial by Rebellion

In today's techno-industrialized society, in a global free market with an excess inventory of knowledge to build deadlier and more sophisticated weaponry, political changes through civil conflicts, military confrontations, and terrorism are not appropriate alternatives to repairing Africa's political stagnation. In the abundance of natural resources and emerging technologies, corruption, fiscal mismanagement, misappropriation of public funds and the lingering shadows of neocolonialism are no longer tenable excuses for the continuity of Africa's misery either.

Part of Africa's economic recovery lies in her stability, building bridges across international and regional trade barriers, gaining access to global investment capital and the compassion of western lending institutions to write off aged debts. African voters also need to support a new crop of technocratic leaders.

At the current rate of technological integration with globalization, it is important to connect Africa's public sector and educational institutions to the technological highway and knowledge base of developed nations.

Finally, there is an urgent need to realign resources to provide sustainable energy, empower local industries, promote the safety and operability of foreign investors, remove complex administrative bureaucracies, prioritize resource allocation and enforce the rule of law.

Acronyms

ECOMOG	Economic Community of West African States Monitoring Group
ECOWAS	Economic Community of West African States
NPFL	National Patriotic Front of Liberia
APC	All Peoples Congress
SLPP	Sierra Leone Peoples Party
ULIMO	United Liberation Movement for Liberia
RUF	Revolutionary United Front
LURD	Liberians United For Reconciliation and Democracy
NPRC	National Provisional Ruling Council
NCO	Non-Commissioned Officer
NUP	National Unity Party
AFL	Armed Forces of Liberia
RPG	Rocket Propelled Grenade
NDPL	National Democratic Party of Liberia
LPC	Liberia Peace Council

RANK	*KIA*	*COMMENTS*
Privates	2,073	Highest other rank casualties
Last Corporals	729	
Corporals	1,038	Highest NCO Casualties
Sergeants	317	
Staff Sergeants	95	
Warrant Officer Class 2	36	
Warrant Officer Class 1	7	Lowest NCO Casualties
Second Lieutenants	12	
Lieutenants	69	Highest Officer Casualties
Captains	10	
Majors	8	
Lieutenants Colonel	1	Lowest Officer casualties
SPECIAL SECURITY DIVISION PERSONNEL		NO DATA AVAILABLE
CIVIL DEFENSE FORCES VIGILANTEES / VOLUNTEERS		NO DATA AVAILBALE
TOTALS	8780	

Made in the USA
Charleston, SC
04 December 2015